You.

Yes, you.

Did the flies

invite you in?

Bug Spray

A Tale of ~~Love~~

~~and~~

Madness

Written by FELIX I.D. DIMARO

Cover artwork by Maev Simard

Typography and Graphic Design by Courtney Swank

ALSO BY
FELIX I.D. DIMARO

How To Make A Monster:
The Loveliest Shade of Red

Warning

This story contains mature content,
including explicit language, adult themes,
gender and racial issues,
scenes depicting graphic violence,
drug use, explicit sex,
self-harm and suicide.

Discretion is advised.

For Courtney, the best "imaginary"
friend a person could ask for

Contents

Part One

Part Two

Post-Mortem

Part One

Suicide

SHE RAGED

i.

"How can you say that about someone who just died? How can you say that about someone you *knew*?" This was Bethany Helmsley. Bethany, Beth, Betts. It depended on who you were and how you knew her. Her boss – the man she was raging at on this gray April day – had called her each of those names depending on where they were and what they were doing. He called her a lot of things.

We'll get there.

On most days she would be described as funny in a way that bordered on raunchy. Lascivious.

On most days, she would be described as friendly, affable, approachable, level-headed. Other admirable qualities.

On most days.

Today was her first day back at work after the death of Reese Mitchell, her favorite co-worker. A guy who, over their four years together working at Helping Hand Home and Auto Insurance, had become her best friend. He had entered her life shortly after her previous best friend – someone she'd known since before she was capable of remembering -– had died of Leukemia following a year-long battle. A Godsend is what Reese had been after that tragedy.

She had prayed and prayed after her previous best friend had died. Prayed to wake up from the living nightmare her life had become. Bethany had prayed and done not much else.

She had taken leave from this same job at Helping Hand Home and Auto Insurance and, each night, had mourned and hoped (and prayed some more) that when she woke up, she would somehow be back to her old life. That hadn't happened.

The darkness that had emerged from the void left by the death of her first best friend had entered directly into her heart. That darkness had spread from her heart, one beat at a time, to the rest of her system, dimming her from the inside.

It had taken every bit of strength she'd had not to relapse into previous bad habits. Returning to the things she had once quit would have been the surest indication she had been quitting on the life she'd fought so hard to build. Elena, Bethany's deceased best friend, wouldn't have wanted that.

Bethany had worked up the courage, with a great deal of effort, to drag herself to work because she had needed the money more than the time to mourn.

She had become convinced that her weeks of prayer had been for nothing until she'd met the new hire. A guy who had only been there for a couple of weeks. Reese, he had said his name was, and smiled kindly at her. It was the smile of a person who understood she wasn't quite where she needed to be. Of a person who would give her the space she needed to get there. He had understood she wasn't where she needed to be because hc too had never quite gotten to a place where he could feel complete, had never gotten to a place where things were okay for him. Somewhere along the line, he'd gotten lost. Lost hope. Stopped believing that he could ever get there.

Suicide.

Reese had restored her hope as their friendship had germinated, but he could never quite find his own. That made it even worse for Bethany (Betts, to Reese). It made her feel guilty, as though somehow this was her fault. As though if she hadn't absorbed so much hope from him right from the start, he might have had some left for himself over the years.

She mourned, she hurt, she looked at the man in front of her at that moment.

She raged.

The man she had just yelled at, and would, in short order, begin screaming at again, was named Tybalt Ward. Referred to as Mr. Ward by those who knew him. Blood relatives excluded. Sexual interests also excluded. Sometimes.

Bethany Helmsley often called him Ty when they were in private. Right now, she was on the verge of calling him many other things, none of which a man of his stature was accustomed to hearing himself referred to as.

This confrontation had started with Mr. Ward approaching Ms. Helmsley – this was one of the many names he would use when speaking to her, though the tone of the name varied depending on the scenario they found themselves in.

Bethany had been at her desk. Mr. Ward had been doing the rounds the way office-types in leadership roles often do. When he approached her desk, he told her that he was glad to see her back at the office, but stated that he didn't understand why she had been gone for so long. The guy – he had referred to poor dead Reese as 'the guy' – had given himself what he'd wanted. At least according to Mr. Ward. He had explained, 'He couldn't handle the world, and now he doesn't have to deal with it'. He'd gone on to argue that he thought people ought to respect suicide the way they respected abortions or Euthanasia. 'Someone made a decision; we should all accept it and move on.'

It was at that point that Bethany had exploded. Questioning how he could say such a thing about someone who had just died, who they had both known. She hadn't added the part she had thought after she had stopped yelling. She hadn't said aloud the thought: *Especially because you know how much he meant to me.*

"Why mourn?" Mr. Ward asked in response to Bethany's outburst of a question. He scoffed, not at all phased by Beth's fury. "This is what he wanted. That's all I'm saying. Tell me, did he love you? Did he love the family and friends that are probably all crying and broken to bits over this situation just like you are right now? Think about it. All I'm saying is that, if he'd loved you and you him, he would want you to understand that this was his limit, he couldn't handle anything else. He wanted to go... I'm not saying you should celebrate, I'm just saying I don't see the point in spending my time crying over the death of someone who wanted to be dead. There are innocents dying all the time. So many that we barely pause to consider them as individuals, let alone mourn them. We don't cry when we hear the stories of those African children who starve to death, or Syrians slaughtered at war, or whoever else you see in news reports we mostly ignore. You don't shed any tears for them, yet you can't get a grip when it comes to someone who *wanted* to be dead. It makes no sense to me."

She said nothing. Silently seething. He continued,

"It's what he wanted... This world is for the strong. Survival of the fittest, remember?"

Survival of the fittest, such a brilliant and revolutionary scientific tenet. Bastardized here. Defiled here. Perverted in this moment of time.

It was the motto of the home and auto insurance sales team of which both Mr. Ward and Bethany were members. Survival of the fittest, a reference to the cutthroat sales competition that was held each month. Theirs was a sales team that emphasized performance over everything else, resulting in immense turnover when it came to the staff. People were hired, people were fired, people quit. The fittest survived.

Mr. Ward had survived and thrived for over two years after taking over from the previous manager when she had suffered a nervous breakdown. Tybalt had used his predecessor's failing mind as a reason to implement this slogan. This creed. He had used the previous sales manager's nervous breakdown as an example during his introductory speech at Helping Hand. Had said that she was the last of the people unfit for this position. That he was going to introduce strength into this office. No room for weakness. Numbers had been lagging, and he knew that they could bring them up if they stayed strong. Fit. Mentally. He had said that anyone who hadn't felt up to the challenge could leave then and there.

One person had stood up, said, 'I don't get paid enough for this shit,' and walked out.

Within four months half the team had been replaced. Betts and Reese had each been the last of their respective groups of trainees. They had made it through the years, proven themselves fit... Until just over a month prior to this confrontation when Reese had taken his life, leaving Betts alone. The survivor. The fittest of survivors. The only one fit enough to tell this walking trash pile exactly what she thought of him.

The remaining members of his team were afraid of Mr. Ward. All afraid of being branded as weak, which, to Bethany, made them the worst kind of weak there could be. *Cowards.*

She looked around at those around them and locked eyes with no one, because everyone's eyes were suddenly finding interesting items to look at all over the office. One set of eyes was fascinated by what must have been the world's most interesting stapler. Another was rivetted by the inside of an empty coffee cup. The carpet must have been especially attractive that day because several sets of eyes examined it as though the bland blue-gray fabric was a piece of fine art.

None of the owners of these eyes moved a muscle, ocular or otherwise. No, they didn't move because there was a show to be experienced. A live drama to be peeked at when the moment was opportune; heard clearly even when it wasn't. Once Bethany had turned her focus back on Mr. Ward, they would lock onto that show, watching and saying nothing, listening carefully in preparation for their eventual repetition of what they would hear, the way cowards usually do. She knew what this muted, mousy crowd would be like in an hour, in a day, in a week.

They would say things such as,

'If he EVER talked to me that way, I would have punched him in the face.'

Like,

'He is SO lucky that wasn't me he was dealing with.'

And,

'She's a much better person than me. I REALLY would have snapped.'

You've heard it before.

But they wouldn't, and he wasn't, and they wouldn't.

All they would have done was cower, cringe, crawl away. They watched now as Bethany was about to do the opposite.

She opened her mouth to rage again...

BEFORE SHE RAGED

i.

This had all started on a coach bus, this thing between Tybalt Ward and Bethany Helmsley. Before all of the raging. Before all of the yelling and goading. They had been adults. Civil.

It had started on a Friday afternoon roughly five months before Bethany made the decision to tell the man she now considered a walking trash pile exactly what she thought of him.

They had been waiting in the office parking lot for a coach bus that would take them to the company's annual summit. Leaving from Daphnis, Washington. Heading to Seattle. It was a drive that generally took roughly an hour-and-a-half.

Every employee of Helping Hand Home and Auto Insurance from all over the Pacific Northwest would be there. The itinerary for the day included the actual conference part of the summit with the usual uplifting *Rah rah rah!* and the *We can do even better next year!,* followed by a dinner, and then by freedom for the night.

Most of the people who didn't live in the Seattle area had chosen to stay at the hotel where the summit was being held. The entire Daphnis office would be staying at the hotel and returning the next morning on the same bus.

There had been rumors, of course, as there always are when it comes to intraoffice overnight gatherings. Rumors of who would be making a play for whom, who would be cheating on their spouse, who might be spending the night with someone they'd have to work awkwardly alongside the Monday after.

There's a thin line between co-worker and Fuck Buddy.

Tybalt was privy to most rumors. He had knowledge of the women in the office who had crossed that line between co-worker and Fuck Buddy. Bethany had been one of them. If the rumors could be believed, she had been with one of the underwriters. The adjacent rumor to this was that she'd chosen to screw the underwriter in order to insure questionable risks. Boost her sales numbers as a result.

Rumors, Tybalt had thought, as everyone milled about in front of the building they shared with about half-a-dozen companies. Though it was only Helping Hand employees who loitered around, waiting to be picked up by a bus that would take them to a weekend of potential greatness, or disaster. No one ever knew which it would be until they were too many drinks in, fueled by the liquid courage which would allow them to attempt to get cozy with the co-worker they'd always secretly fancied. Or whichever staff member looked equal parts good and good to go in the moment.

Mr. Ward had looked over at Bethany, who had been engaged in conversation with a few others from his sales team. It was an odd group to observe, he thought. Though office friend groups usually make for motley crews. Along with Bethany was Heath Carlton, a hulking man in his mid-twenties. He had flowing copper hair and muscles that made his work attire look like body art. Edith Myers was in the group as well; a middle-aged and slightly overweight woman that the young brokers in the office lovingly referred to as 'mom'. And, of course, because Bethany was in this grouping, so too was Reese Mitchell. The two took turns acting as each other's shadow. If Reese hadn't spent so much of his time openly flirting with Heath, Tybalt may have thought something was going on between the short, thin thirty-something and Bethany. Bethany, who was the only person in the group that Tybalt had any genuine interest in on that day.

There had been a random draw to determine seating partners for the trip – a suggestion made by Dagny Cole, the Assistant Human Resources Officer – as a way to encourage new relationships that might foster new ideas and greater morale. Morale had dropped when that announcement had been made. It had plummeted further when the pairings had been called out. Tybalt and Bethany had been the last two seating partners named.

He had looked at her as she chatted with her teammates, waiting for the bus. Gazed surreptitiously, attempted to solve her in his mind. He couldn't picture the rumors about her being true, mainly because she looked so... plain. Unassuming. She had short hair and dark features, was average height, slim, harmless-looking. Unspectacular by certain standards. But he knew better than most that looks could be deceiving. There was much more to her than there seemed, he was certain of it, and had thought to himself that this might be a good time to find out just how much more. He had been excited at the prospect.

It wasn't just the potential for crossing lines and breaking boundaries that made Tybalt look forward to events like these. These festivities gave him a chance to strut, to preen, to network. To shatter expectations and take credit for all of his hard work.

Bethany had felt the exact opposite, wanting to slink into the shadows and be ignored until this thing came to an end. The fact that she would have to spend the entire drive sitting beside Mr. Ward didn't help her apprehension and anxiety about the event. The two had known each other for several years now, but had only really spoken in the office, talking about office-related issues. Exchanging forced laughter while sharing the sort of uncomfortable conversations that only exist between underling and boss.

When the coach bus had pulled up, the staff proceeded to pass along their baggage from hand to hand to hand until it was safely stowed in the luggage compartment at the side of the bus.

After handing off her luggage to Reese, Bethany had turned to make her way to the door and spotted her bus buddy, Mr. Ward, looking at her. They exchanged an uncomfortable smile. She turned back to Reese a final time before proceeding to the bus, toward Mr. Ward. Reese had mouthed 'good luck' and winked at her. She had tried to not visibly cringe in response, in case Mr. Ward was still looking her way. She had always regarded him as a stiff, pompous, just-tolerable, untrustworthy man whose entire being made it seem like he was overcompensating for some inferiority complex. While most of the other males headed to the summit wore nothing fancier than a shirt and tie, Mr. Ward wore a midnight blue three-piece suit with a stark white pocket square spilling wildly and very un-square-like from his breast pocket. He was clean shaven, as always, his brown skin flawlessly smooth, and she couldn't recall ever having seen him without what looked like a fresh haircut. She couldn't understand why he always had to try so hard.

Beth had looked at his pristine suit before staring at her own outfit. She scrutinized her plain forest green sheath dress and white ballet flats. Suddenly wishing she had put on something else. Something better. She would have a chance to change at the hotel before the dinner, but what she had brought as a backup outfit wasn't much of an improvement. Mr. Ward made her feel insecure. He had always made her feel insecure.

Thinking of the trip to come, she hoped that he was a reader, or, even better, an audiobook enthusiast. That he would fill in the crossword or play Sudoku, or do anything that would create a silence between them that wouldn't be uncomfortable. A reasonable silence. Anything that ensured the two of them would not have to communicate while not noticing how much they did not want to communicate.

She had looked his way again, surprised to find that he was still looking in her direction. At her.

They had done the thing people do when unexpected eye contact is made. The thing where eyes dart and shift and look everywhere, at nothing, at anything, not wanting to be caught staring after obviously already having been caught staring. The two of them had done that before glancing at each other again, then boarding the bus. He had tried her once more with a tentative smile. In that smile, Beth had read the same apprehension she was feeling. She had thought he probably didn't want to sit next to her any more than she wanted to sit next to him.

Tybalt had flashed her a smile he hoped didn't make him seem too eager. A smile that wouldn't betray just how badly he actually did want to sit next to her.

Sit together they did. After boarding, she had realized, to her chagrin, that he wasn't a reader or an audiobook enthusiast, or a Sudoku player. He was a meditator. And he was meditating beside her.

Initially, she'd thought he had fallen asleep, until she realized that his breathing had a very regular rhythm, a controlled pattern. His meditation was confirmed when she saw that his hands were sitting neatly in his lap, the forefingers and thumbs of each hand connected together in a way that seemingly signalled to his legs that everything was okay.

Bethany had found herself becoming fascinated by this. She had sometimes referred to herself as a wannabe hippie, spending time talking about the many amazing benefits of yoga, but rarely doing it. Speaking of the usefulness of meditation, but only in theory and almost never in practice. She recycled though, and she was proud of that.

Watching Mr. Always-in-a-suit-never-being-compassionate-only-caring-about-survival-of-the-fittest doing something so grounded, so down to earth, as meditating, made her see him in a beautiful and different light. She'd found herself staring at him. Trying to absorb that unfamiliar illumination which had surrounded him at that moment.

She'd been playing that risky game – her reflexes versus his eyelids. The one where she would lose if he opened his eyelids and her reflexes weren't fast enough to avoid making it seem as though she had been staring at him like a fucking creeper the entire time his eyes had bee–

His eyes had opened without warning.

She'd tried to look away, but it was about a second later than she should have. He'd won the game of his eyelids versus her reflexes.

His prize, he had decided, would be an attempt to make awesome conversation.

Her punishment, she had feared, would be him making awkward conversation.

"I'm sorry." She hadn't known what else to say as he gazed at her. She had turned red under his scrutiny. "I'm just... when did you start to meditate? I've always wanted to do it, but I've never had the patience for it." Her voice had been barely audible over the engine, the sounds of the road seeping in all around them, and the excited chatter of the other passengers on the bus.

"Do you have the patience for it right now?" he'd asked before giving her a curious grin. An expression unlike any she had ever seen upon his face as he trotted around the office or while he grimaced at his computer screen for hours at a time. He had seemed almost amiable just then, almost approachable on a person-to-person level despite the professional dynamic between them.

Before she could respond to his question, he'd twisted in his seat and placed his hands on her shoulders, positioning her so that her back was flat against her seat. Then he had put her hands on her knees before assuming the same position.

"Do I have to do the 'okay' sign thing with my hands?" she'd asked.

He had looked at her curiously until she held up her hands, putting both thumbs and both forefingers together, holding each hand up and flashing the universal hand sign for 'a-okay'. He'd understood. Chuckled. Shaken his head. Said,

"No. You just have to keep your hands still in whatever position you decide to put them in when you begin your meditation. That's the first thing you need to know, how to be still. To let things be as they are even if you can't move to change them. Your body has to be still to let you know that, even if you can't react or do anything to change what is happening around you, it's okay. It's okay to just accept things as they are before you let them go."

She had accepted this and was still.

"Close your eyes."

She did.

"When you exhale, focus on your upper lip. Feel the air as it passes over. Concentrate on that air, let anything that enters your mind exit it like the air from your nostrils over your lip. Nothing else matters but your breath. Focus on that, my voice, and nothing else."

She did that too.

ii.

Mr. Ward had spoken to Bethany that way for several minutes, telling her how to breathe, how to focus on her breathing. Guiding her meditation, putting her at ease.

From her, exorcising control. Upon her, exercising control.

And, once she'd gotten over the fact that she shouldn't possibly have been able to feel this tranquil on a bus full of coworkers while her boss, the least people-person person there ever was, whispered in her ear, telling her how to breathe – once she'd gotten over all of that – she was perhaps as relaxed as she had ever been in her life.

She had put her hand on his forearm seconds after he'd told her that it was time to open her eyes. Open her eyes and see if she saw things a little differently than the lifetime ago that had been the five minutes in which he had been guiding her. The lifetime ago crammed within the five minutes that felt like a few seconds. When you start to feel something for someone you thought it was impossible to ever feel feelings for, everything, including time, suddenly has a way of not making much sense. Of being warped. Twisted.

Their eyes had met. Locked. And somehow this had made her feel freer than she had in years. She'd looked into his dark brown eyes and seen that it was her and him – the work stuff, their roles, where they were coming from and going to, it all billowed away like litter in a windstorm. She had seen beauty in those eyes where she had previously only seen hardness and an eagerness to discipline. With her hand on his arm and his eyes on her eyes, she'd said,

"Wow. Mr. Ward... I wasn't expecting that. Thank you. How did you learn such a skill?" There had been flirtation there, traces of it. But she had also been using her 'I'm speaking to my boss' tone. A tone of voice that anyone who knew her outside of work would likely have mocked and teased her for. She had used that tone in case her flirtatiousness was misguided. She had used it to gauge his reaction to what she had said. She used the tone in hopes that he would give her a sign that she could perhaps stop using it going forward.

He had paused. Looked at her intently as if deciding whether or not to share a thing he did not quite feel comfortable sharing. She had tried to goad him on, to encourage him with just her eyes and her stillness, hoping she was projecting the fact that she was receptive and non-judgmental. He seemed to decide. After a sigh, he said,

"My dad died pretty early on in my life. He died at war. I was ten when it happened... After that, it was just me, my mom and my little sister. I used to act out. So, my mom called her dad because she thought I needed a father figure in my life. A man, you know? She had that old-fashioned way of thinking that a mother can't raise a well-adjusted child without a man to help her. Anyway, it put my mom at ease for me to spend two weekends a month with my grandfather in order to get my head on straight. She hadn't realized that my grandfather had become quite the hippie. He was... more eccentric with me than he let on when the entire family was together." Mr. Ward had broken their gaze as he'd gotten further into his story and, only after announcing what his grandfather was, did he lock eyes with her again. He chuckled, giving her permission to smile, to try to do the same. Giving her permission to breathe, which she hadn't been doing until that point. She relaxed again. Took in air, let it out. He continued his story.

"My grandpa would smoke what he called 'special cigs'. Boys' stuff. No one was supposed to know about them. Especially not 'mommies'. Then we would go out back of his house – his backyard bordered the woods – and we would practice sling-shooting. He'd made me a slingshot and told me it was more secret boys' stuff." He chuckled again and shook his head wistfully. His expression allowed her to see the boy he had once been, and suddenly she couldn't imagine how she had ever thought of him as a hardened man. A sourpuss. "Those weekends went on for a couple of years." Mr. Ward continued. "He died when I was twelve. It wasn't until I was sixteen before I realized that my grandfather was getting stoned and doing dumb kid shit with me while he was trying to figure out how to tell his daughter and two grandkids that he had terminal cancer." He paused at this part.

He always paused at this part.

She did the things that he was used to seeing whenever he told people this story. Her back hunched a little. Her shoulders slumped. She forgot how to use her eyelids. She uttered a sound of sympathy that he couldn't be certain was a word rather than a grunt. It didn't really matter, he understood her. He went on.

"One of the things my grandfather taught me, before he really started to deteriorate, was how to meditate. How to really keep control of myself and my temper. I remember asking him if his special cigs might help with that. He told me 'not until you're old as I am, son.' He always called me 'son'...

"We eventually got around to talking about life and death. We didn't talk about his cancer specifically, but he sometimes spoke about being old. Coming closer to death while growing further from being one of the living. I thought of my dad then, and I asked how my grandfather dealt with it – with death in general, and with the potential of his specifically. What he said was that meditation was one of the few things that gave him peace of mind. It made him remember that what is is, and what can't be never will be. And sometimes that's all there is to life. It's sort of bleak advice, especially to hear as a kid, but it really helps you when you're trying to shut out all of the external and focus only on the things you can control."

She was baffled. Here was this guy who she had thought of as a stone, suddenly removing his hard exterior and showing her layers she would never have guessed could have existed. She looked at him, up and down and back again. He seemed like an entirely new creature to her. Bethany understood this must have been a difficult story to tell, but, somehow, she had brought something out of him. A sharing quality that was so out of his character. And, much to her ever-growing surprise, he seemed content on continuing to share.

They talked.

The entire bus ride, they talked.

When the bus finally stopped at the site of the summit, they'd continued to talk as they got off. Conversed as, hand by hand by hand, their luggage was passed to them.

Finally, it was time for them to go their separate ways. They didn't quite know what to do then, because they wanted to continue talking. Though whether they would do so depended upon the next thing either of them would say. It was Bethany who spoke first, and the words she heard from her own mouth shocked her.

"Meet back in the lobby in a half hour?" she asked, then, looking his fancy suit up and down, added, "Or do you need more time?"

She was relieved when he laughed. Even more so when he agreed to meet back at the lobby in half an hour after they had checked in, put away their luggage and done whatever they needed to do before they sat down at the summit for the *Rah rah rah!*.

iii.

After that half hour had passed, they'd met in the lobby, continuing their conversation immediately upon seeing each other again, even before they were within earshot of one another. Eventually they were side by side, then stride by stride, walking and talking to and into the summit which was being held in the party room of the hotel they had just checked into.

He didn't strut. He didn't preen. He didn't schmooze.

She didn't worry about awkward small talk with people who would only be speaking to her in hopes of some networking opportunity. Some chance to spread the company cheer. There was none of that, because it was her and him and nothing about their talk was small.

Unfortunately, their talk was short-lived. The two were separated by poor seating plans, people who needed Mr. Ward's attention, and awards. Particularly the award for Most Improved Sales Team, which Mr. Ward had graciously accepted on behalf of the Daphnis team, winking at Bethany as he had bounded off the stage.

Betts flushed as Reese and the others wondered aloud what had put the pep into their manager's step.

Mr. Ward and Bethany stole a word from one another here and there throughout the night, but were eventually separated by the owner and Chief Executive Officer of the company, one Mr. Henry Johjima. This was an interruption that Tybalt was pleased with (even as a part of him lamented watching Bethany walk away). He went from being pleased to being near elated once he'd learned that the tycoon had made a point of seeking Tybalt out to invite him for a drink. He revered Mr. Johjima. The Japanese business mogul was one of the very few men that Tybalt allowed himself to refer to with words such as 'idol' or 'hero'. He was honored to be in the man's company.

Words like 'congratulations' and 'great job' and 'wonderful new direction' were used by Mr. Johjima regarding Tybalt's performance. The two men celebrated, drank. And Tybalt was so enthralled with being able to pick the brain of his idol, live and in color, that at least an hour had passed by before he noticed that Bethany had left the party. He scanned the room time and time again but never saw her.

He rued that she was gone. Rued it vigorously though internally because he had to keep up appearances for Mr. Johjima, had to be raptly engaged, responsive at all times. Most importantly, he had to let Mr. Johjima continue talking until the businessman ended the conversation. Tybalt knew that it would be taken as a sign of utmost disrespect if he brushed the owner of the company off for anything other than a death in the family.

Mr. Johjima talked about politics and insurance trends, even baseball. He talked about everything that wasn't Bethany Helmsley. Eventually, thankfully, Mr. Johjima excused himself. A few minutes later Tybalt saw the business mogul schmoozing with another rising sales captain from a different branch of Helping Hand. He wondered if perhaps the aging owner and CEO was scoping out potential replacements for himself down the line. If so, he was elated to be in the running.

At times like this– times of success and accomplishment – Tybalt thought back to his youth. To sitting at the breakfast table eating gruel with his mother and little sister. The three of them drinking tea, sharing the same bag. His mother having nothing because, as she had explained to Ty and his sister for years, she had run through the little compensation given to the wife of a soldier who gave his life for his country. His dad, the fallen soldier. Tybalt scoffed at the memory of that.

He thought back to meals which consisted of ham and sliced bread. Of cheese and sliced bread. He recalled how everything from a hot dog to a hamburger, from peanut butter and jelly to a thin slice of Spam, how so many vile things fit so perfectly onto sliced white bread. Oh, how Tybalt Ward loathed sliced white bread now. Now that he had supped upon many of life's true delicacies.

He gave Mr. Johjima one last glance, almost hungrily, and knew that there would be even finer dining ahead. If he played his cards right.

Tybalt had retreated into his thoughts, calculating just what those cards might be and how they could be played. He leaned against the drink station, elbows on the bar, eyes drowning in the clear liquid inside his glass.

He heard everyone around him, colleagues, competitors, thin lines between them all. He heard them in the way a person hears things they aren't listening to. They had become chatter, murmurs, the **tinks** and **clinks** of glassware and silverware and fine china and fine everything that Tybalt was trying to figure out how to make his own. So deep in thought was Tybalt that he barely registered it when actual words broke through the din. Words aimed at him.

"You looking for something in the bottom of that drink, Mr. Ward?" Tybalt looked up, looked over to his left at the source of the sound, kept his face as straight as possible.

Give away nothing, he'd thought to himself as he looked into the green eyes of the slender brunette sitting on the barstool beside him.

This was Mantra 24 of the Mantras of Tybalt Ward. *33 Mantras for Mindfulness and Mastery* was a book Tybalt had picked up around the same time he'd begun to meditate. He treated it as his own personal Bible.

He gave away nothing of himself as he pondered the question asked by the attractive stranger beside him. What had Tybalt been looking for at the bottom of his drink? A solution? That must have been it. A solution that would lead to all of the things he wanted in this world. *Give away nothing,* he repeated the mantra internally while smirking at the woman. He responded,

"Actually, the drink was talking to me. It was just telling me that I needed some company before I could drink it. It said it's not the type of drink that gets drunk by guys who drink alone." Sometimes he babbled, Tybalt did. This was part of his strategy. He found that if you said enough words of almost any nature while well-dressed and good-looking, women would find a way to make their own sense of those words. Find a way to make it a compliment of some sort. Turn those words into something that intrigued them at the very least.

She laughed at his string of nonsense. He immediately began to calculate, which was Mantra Number 3:

Calculate. Analyze what has happened; formulate what happens next.

By his calculation, just based upon her approaching him and starting off the conversation, he was already more than halfway there. Halfway to her. Practically in her.

He observed her. Tybalt Ward rarely ever only looked, he observed. He saw her with her curly hair. Hair that she probably described as chestnut or chocolate or deep bronze even though it was really just brown. He observed that, when she laughed, she tilted her head back. Her hand touched her chin. She brushed locks of curly brown hair off her collar bone, behind her shoulders, fully revealing quite the décolletage.

More than three quarters of the way there.

"Well then, let's not make you a guy who drinks alone. There's nothing sadder than a drink that goes... undrunk? Is that right? Undrunken?... A drink that isn't consumed." She giggled again, and Tybalt sensed a bit of embarrassment in that giggle. She had stumbled, and that broke through the veneer of badass who approaches bigshot at the bar. This meant she would be eager to redeem herself. Eager for affirmation. Approval. He laughed a laugh that sounded purposely false. He shifted away from her, only slightly, but enough for her to notice. Whether consciously or subconsciously, he'd known she would pick up on it. And, because she had started this and she had stumbled on her words when she'd put herself out there, she would react.

She put her hand on his arm.

Eighty Percent.

"What are we drinking to?" she asked.

The barman walked over right on cue, looked at both of them expectantly. The woman looked at Tybalt, Tybalt looked at her, arched an eyebrow. The look said, 'What do you want?'. And she didn't know whether he meant what drink she wanted, or the 'What do you want?' that means, 'Get the fuck out of here'.

She had briefly, in a moment of abject horror, wondered if she was being asked to leave. And that's when, to the bartender, Tybalt said,

"Two of whatever the lady is having." Then, to her, "We're drinking to potential."

She turned back to him; her face was flushed but that flush was fading. She was settling herself down, still looking for redemption. She looked at the drink in front of Tybalt, barely turned to the bartender, pointed at the drink and said,

"Two of those."

The barman looked from the woman to Tybalt, as if needing affirmation. Tybalt gave him a look that said, 'Why are you still here?', and then the bartender was not there. Wanting his tip, he went to tend bar with immediacy. The brunette, who was now practically leaning on Tybalt, spoke into his ear.

"We can drink to all kinds of potentials."

Nine-tenths of the way there.

It was just a matter of closing. Agreeing on a time and a place. Duration and location.

"I have drinks in my room," Tybalt had responded. She'd smiled at him with her lips as well as her big green eyes. Tybalt wondered what she would look like when those eyes were rolled up into her head, making little green crescent moons below her upper eyelids. Her nose flaring slightly. Her mouth in an 'O' as they did the thing that human bodies were made to do.

He stood. She stood.

He had pictured all of the things that their two bodies, which were practically created to be intertwined, could do. It had almost hurt him to look at her long lean frame. She was nearly six feet tall, almost matching his own height, a rarity for him. Tybalt hoped he wouldn't regret his decision. The decision not to explore this any further even though they were only about ten percent – an elevator ride and a layer of clothing – away from being one-hundred percent there. Still, he'd had a feeling. Not necessarily a feeling about this girl, but about another. And the feeling he was feeling about that other girl made all the feelings he felt for this one seem wrong.

He sighed, genuinely disappointed. The bartender brought over the drinks. Tybalt paid him, making sure to tip more than was necessary. He picked up the gin and tonic he had previously been nursing when his thoughts had been interrupted by the brunette woman. Finished it in a gulp. Set his glass down. Said,

"We'll be drinking to potential unrealized... separately. I have drinks in my room, but I hope these drinks suffice for you."

He had turned even before he could see her reaction, though he could have imagined it well enough. And, even as he walked away, he braced himself for some potential attack from her. Drinks thrown at him, maybe. Even worse, the glasses which held those drinks. Worse yet, her throwing herself at him in a much more physical way than she had just done. But there was no attack.

He never turned back. Tybalt imagined her standing there, nursing those drinks. Staring into them. Eventually someone would ask her what she was looking for in there, and she would likely say, 'Someone to share this second drink with', and then she would have the night she wanted. At that moment, he had to follow his feeling.

iv.

It was an hour after getting to his room before some doubt began to set into Tybalt's mind. He began to wonder if maybe he should head back to the hotel bar and find the tall girl with the lean body and the curly brown hair. Tell her that the potential between them could be realized. Tell her that he realized the mistake he'd made by walking away. That he could make it up to her. But he held off. She was probably already engaged in some activity with someone else. Plus, his feeling was still there, telling him to wait.

While he waited, he drank those drinks he had in his room and watched an old episode of *Friends*. There was a marathon of the show broadcasting on one of those stations that had, once upon a time, played music videos. The episode was *The One with The Ring,* where Chandler is getting ready to propose to Monica, and hijinks ensue. He had never understood the fascination with the show, but he had flipped through all the channels on the hotel television and this was it. He once again wondered if he'd done the right thing. Made the right choice. He was about to start repeating Mantra 21:

The word risk is the word risk for a reason. Don't beat yourself up for being bold.

It was after 1 AM when he had been about to make peace with the way his night had gone. Then there was a knock on the door. So soft was the sound that he thought he might have been imagining it.

Tybalt got up from the hotel bed, checked himself in the mirror a final time, put in a breath strip, and walked to the door. The feeling that had been so strong earlier swelled.

He opened the door and his feeling was confirmed.

There she was.

Bethany.

All feelings had been about her.

"Bethany. I'm... I hoped you would show up. It's a shame we didn't get to sit together during dinner, or talk after it. I truly enjoyed the conversation we had on the bus ride here... and after it." This was as much vulnerability as he ever allowed himself to show.

This was a side of Tybalt Ward that Bethany Helmsley had never expected to see, had never believed existed. She believed it now as she saw him there, wearing a t-shirt and pajama pants, his hair as disheveled as she had ever seen it, his eyes surprised but happy in a way that she thought her eyes mirrored in that moment. Happy in a way that said, 'I don't believe what I'm seeing but I want to keep seeing it'.

"I wanted to keep seeing you. Sorry... I mean, I wanted to see you. I... I can't sleep. And I keep thinking about our conversation on the bus and how you made me relax so easily, and I was hoping you could make me relax again."

He didn't want to calculate where he was with her. He simply let the feeling that had guided them both there be the feeling that would lead them from then onward.

"Of course. I'd like nothing more." He gestured for her to enter. She entered. She removed her shoes and they walked toward the King-sized bed in the middle of the suite. She wore a red sweater that said Washington State across the front in bold white letters. He couldn't help but notice, as she walked ahead of him, how her gray pajama bottoms clung to her shape, highlighting her hips and ass and making him second guess his earlier thoughts of her as unassuming, plain.

The television was on, but the volume was turned to a mumble. Paperwork was spread all over the hotel desk. A laptop was open displaying a white screen with black words that looked like nothing Bethany would want to be reading on a Friday night. He saw the look she was giving the desk and computer and knew that some damage control was in order. He didn't want her to think of him as her boss. Not tonight. Not right now. He went to speak, but she made it so he wouldn't have to.

"I saw you with Mr. Johjima," she said. "I figured he would have you talking business, but I didn't realize he would put you to work like this. This whole thing was supposed to be about celebration and relaxing. Just more Helping Hand bullshit." Then she caught herself, eyes flaring, hand over her mouth to stop any more idiocy that might squeeze past her lips.

She had forgotten that she was talking to her boss (much as Tybalt had hoped), though the words she had released brought the reminder of their dynamic rumbling into the room like a large pink elephant. She had no idea how Mr. Ward would react to slanderous talk about Helping Hand Home and Auto Insurance. From everything she could tell, he was a company man. He'd spent most of the evening chatting with the owner and all of the higher-ups for God's sake. How could she have been so stupid?

"Yeah, as you can see, they don't actually offer much in terms of a helping hand." He said this with a smirk. And she laughed in sheer relief at his joke. He smiled at her warmly, gestured toward the desk. "But it's fine. If you want to move up, you have to put in the hard work." For a moment the elephant, which had made its way out of the room, poked its head back around the corner. But it was quickly shooed away.

"But you're right." Tybalt said, still smiling at her, "This weekend is all about celebration." He shut down his laptop, closed the physical files on the table, gestured for her to sit on the bed.

She sat. He sat.

They talked.

About her and him and all things related. She told him things that she could have never imagined talking to him about. About her wayward brother, her dead parents, how she wound up in insurance, and even how much she hated what they did for a living. She left out her own demons, the worst of her past. The demons that still haunted her younger brother. This was still her boss after all, and she couldn't risk revealing too much. The situation was delicate enough already.

However, it didn't feel as though she was speaking to her boss when he reciprocated, telling her more about being the man of the house when he was just a boy. About how, before he had died, Tybalt's militaristic father had drilled discipline into him, and how he had carried that, out of both guilt and respect, into his adulthood. Explained to her that he understood why people mistook him for a hard man. Told her he was simply a man of discipline, and hoped she could understand that. She said she could. Back and forth they went. Serve. Volley. Volley. Serve.

For hours they talked, until all at once it seemed as though all of the words in all of the world had been exhausted between the two of them, and neither could find a single one to say.

It seemed that, with the extinction of words, they would have to communicate non-verbally.

With their bodies.

They talked.

V.

This entire thing, the thing between Bethany and Tybalt, was like a whirlwind with its suddenness and unpredictability. It swept them up like a tornado. Shook their worlds like an earthquake. Other natural disasters apply.

The morning after that first night was what cemented the fact that this wouldn't be a one-time thing. In fact, Bethany thought, after she had gotten dressed and walk-of-shamed it back to her own suite, the next time they would do the act would make it a five-time thing.

They had done it twice before they'd passed out. Twice more after she'd woken him with her hand and a light squeeze in the right spot three short hours later. There would have been a third time that morning, but the later she stayed, the more she increased the risk of her running into someone on her way out, and maybe having to explain to some busybody why she was on that floor, coming out of that room, looking so disheveled. And, no matter what she might have said, her smile would have given it all away, because she simply could not stop making that expression.

Her life suddenly felt very strange, like the natural order of things had shifted, been reshuffled. There was confusion and uncertainty, but there was also excitement. A lot of it. She had practically floated on that excitement as she made her way back to her room.

vi.

Bethany's excitement diminished only once she got back to her room, sat on the bed and wondered, *What next?* She had no clue what to do or how to behave going forward. She and Tybalt would have to take the bus back to Daphnis from Seattle, and what if they didn't have anything to talk about? What would happen when they got back home? Would she text him? Call him? Add him to her social media? Should she wait for him to do those things? And what if he didn't? What if he was having second thoughts now that she wasn't beside him? What if he avoided her entirely when Monday rolled around? What if he was made so uncomfortable by her presence that he found a way to fire her? These doubts and worries continued to drill their way into her mind, excavating from it her reason, filling the vacated area with anxiety and apprehension.

Her worries only deepened when she didn't see Mr. Ward at the continental breakfast that morning. A couple of hours later, when it was time to board the bus back to Daphnis, she found that she suddenly had extra elbow room. Her bus buddy was nowhere to be found.

Members of her sales team – Reese, Edith, friends of hers – would take turns coming to sit with her from time to time, none of them knowing where their boss was. All of them noting how lucky Bethany was for not having to sit with him all the way back. None of them quite understanding why she wasn't responding with sheer joy.

If they'd only known.

She had made an excuse about an upset stomach to each of them and was left alone with her thoughts for most of the bus ride home.

vii.

By Monday morning she was a wreck. Bethany had stumbled into the office on three hours sleep. She was ten minutes late, blurry eyed, coffee in hand, with a look on her face that said she didn't want to talk to anyone. Sleep usually came extremely easily for Bethany, so she had been as surprised as she had been irritated when she'd spent most of the previous night tossing and turning, wondering why he hadn't reached out, wondering what that would mean for her. For them. She'd spent most of the night scolding herself for having gone to his hotel room. What good had she thought would come of that?

She got to her cubicle, sat at her desk and braced herself for the worst. Usually, she would turn to Reese on mornings when she felt especially stressed. His cubicle was next to hers, but it was empty on this day. She remembered that he was taking the morning off. While they both hated most Mondays, Mondays after an office gathering were particularly unbearable and were to be avoided entirely if at all possible. She kicked herself for not taking the day off as well.

Part of her was relieved that Reese wasn't there that morning, because she didn't want to deal with anyone who knew her as well as he did asking her what was wrong, especially with things going the way they were going. She would have broken down if Reese had been there to ask her that question, she was certain. And she wouldn't have known how to explain to him why she was so full of tears.

Not sure what to do, Bethany briefly considered packing up her things and leaving, but she couldn't imagine just walking out of this place. She hated the job, but she struggled to think of what she would be without this role, this title, this place to go to everyday. Eventually, she put her head in her hands and just sat there.

"Bethany?"

Bethany barely moved. It wasn't the voice she wanted to hear. It was probably the last voice she wanted to hear. It was nasally, condescending and, on a day like this, it was the equivalent of somebody flicking her earlobe with their finger with each word that was spoken. *Flick*. It grated on her in a way that was annoying, near painful.

"Are you okay, Bethany?... Bethany?" *Flick*.

"Yes, Dagny. Christ. Yes, I'm fine. Just a bit of a headache." *Which you're not making any better by chirping at me. Get out of here already,* Bethany thought, hoped, prayed for with her head still in her hands.

Dagny Cole did not get out of there. Bethany could feel her presence. Hovering. About to say more words.

"Bethany." *Flick.* "Mr. Ward would like to see you in his office."

Flick, flick, flick, flick, flick, flick, flick.

Bethany wanted to scream. Instead, she focused on her breathing, and oh how it burned her that even the act of breathing would now, and perhaps forevermore, make her think of him. She slowly removed her face from her hands, looked at Dagny and went to speak, hoping her voice wouldn't betray how terrified and confused she felt. She had hoped to sound aloof. Instead, her voice was meek, uncertain.

"Do I need to bring my things?" The sentence sounded like it was coming from someone else, somewhere else, each word chipped and cracked, her voice a breaking thing.

Dagny was the Assistant Human Resources Officer. The person whose wonderful idea it had been for the team to select random bus buddies. She was the go-between for Human Resources and the various Managers on the sales and service floors. She knew who was coming and going. Sometimes she would come to collect those who were to be fired and bring them to those who did the firing, like The Grim Reaper carrying some poor soul to its maker. Bethany and her coworkers called her The Thin Reaper behind her back on account of the nature of her duties and the slightness of her frame. They all dreaded seeing her walking along the sales floor, sometimes making small talk, sometimes plucking people up to deliver their lives into devastation. You could never tell what was coming with Dagny, she always maintained the same annoying pleasant-seeming disposition.

The Thin Reaper had now set herself on Bethany, it seemed, and Bethany didn't know whether to cling to her desk and politely demand to be dragged out, or to gather what she could and run out without having to see Mr. Ward, the man who had occupied nearly every single one of her thoughts since she had walked out of his hotel room nearly forty-eight hours prior.

What a difference one weekend can make.

She wished for a moment that she could take it all back, but then she considered their day and night together. She remembered the things that he'd done when he'd told her to lay back and let go as he had inched down her body with his lips and his hands and his tongue. She also thought of all of the talking he did to her, with her, with that same talented tongue. How attentive he had been. How open, how vulnerable. How so much of that Friday-into-Saturday had felt like the fairy tales that she had stopped believing were for her since she had accepted that heartbreak was a reality of life. The two – fairy tale endings and heartbreak – couldn't coexist in the world as it was interpreted by Bethany's mind. Since she knew heartbreak firsthand, and had only hoped for fairy tale endings, she had dismissed the idea of the latter altogether, much as she had shed herself of her beliefs in Santa Claus, Leprechauns, the Tooth Fairy. Those types.

The idea of true love seemed to belong more to that grouping of imaginary creatures than it did to that of the concrete things in life she could see and feel and be certain of. She had let her guard down, believing their Friday-into-

Saturday tryst was a real and concrete thing, only for a lonely and uncertain Sunday, and now this very bleak Monday morning, to shatter those beliefs.

"Bethany?" *Flick.* "Are you sure you're okay? Why would you think you'd need to pack up your things? It's the first Monday of the month. You're scheduled for your Targets Meeting in Mr. Ward's office. And you're five minutes late. I was walking past his office and he asked me to remind you."

"Oh." Bethany didn't know what to say, suddenly remembering why she hadn't taken this Monday off. "Thank you," she managed to blurt out.

"No problem! Enjoy your day!" Dagny's voice was like a punch in the throat when it got that high in pitch and volume. She walked away, leaving Bethany alone with her thoughts. Alone before she had to rush to be inside of a room with Mr. Ward. The man who had made their intercourse feel more like they were interlocking. Intertwining.

As Bethany kicked herself for forgetting yet another MTM – Monthly Targets Meeting – she could hear the grating voice of Dagny Cole a few cubicles down from her. Reaping.

"Mindy? Would you mind coming with me to Human Resources? Just a quick chat."

Bethany vaguely heard Mindy start to cry a few cubicles over as she had gathered her notebook and pen and skittered over to Mr. Ward's office, knowing just how much he hated anyone being late.

viii.

"You're late." Mr. Ward. His two words pierced the air. He wasn't pleased, not judging from the look on his face. Or the tone of his voice. Or the body language he displayed. Body language in which she had been so fluent just nights prior.

She wanted to run and hide. She also wanted to grab his face and kiss it until it looked as happy as it had when they'd kissed goodbye two days prior. She had, internally, all of the ingredients required to create deep conflict. Dissonance. All of that conflict boiling inside of her made her doubt her first thought, then the second. The third. Fifty-third. She just stood there, the only thing she trusted was her silence. He responded with the same. Then, after the silence became too loud, she said,

"I'm sorry." She could have given him an excuse, could have lied, made something up, but she didn't believe in being dishonest. And she didn't want to say the truth because it would have come out as, *I'm late because I was thinking about how good our conversation was. I'm late because I was thinking about how our bodies fit together like they were manufactured to be two halves of a whole being, separated by accident. I'm late because I felt like you and me and you in me made so much sense in the moment. It hadn't made sense before or after and I just don't know how to deal with that. I want things to make sense again. That's why I'm late.*

She didn't say any of that, of course. She simply stood, waiting to be reprimanded, still wondering if she'd have to collect her things.

She knew how much Mr. Ward hated when people were late, she didn't know how he reacted when people were late after a weekend tryst. Once again, she considered just turning and walking. But, in her mind, that process translated to the word 'hightailing' and phrases of a similar meaning, such as: running away; for example: tucking one's tail between one's legs, being a coward. Those phrases made her feel greatly ashamed of wanting to walk away when she had done nothing wrong. Still, she had to fight against the urge, simply because she knew that walking away, hightailing or not, would have been much simpler. She didn't walk. She stood. She waited. And then Mr. Ward spoke again.

"You know how much I hate it when people are late."

She froze there, not knowing what response was appropriate. She was unmoving, thinking of a trillion words, yet none of those individual words seemed to want to combine with any other in order to create a sentence. Putting forth her best impersonation of a statue, she stood there with her eyes watery, teary, rheumy, saddened. Maddened. Those eyes screamed at him, W*hy didn't you call me? Why are you treating me like this now? Why are you pretending that none of what happened, happened?*

But she said nothing. And he said nothing. Until he spoke, and said something that said everything.

"Why didn't you call me?" was what he said. She was so flabbergasted by the question and its timing that she took that moment to sit in the chair opposite him. Her knees were too weak for her to stand.

"Why didn't *you* call *me*?" she retorted after most of her composure had returned to her. The surrealness of his question had jarred her completely. She was thankful she was able to simply parrot it back at him and not truly address it.

"It's impolite to answer a question with a question." His lip twitched as he made the effort not to smile.

Fuck, she thought. And the way he allowed himself to smile just then, you would think he'd heard her cursing. He stood up, which, for some reason, she took as a sign that she should stand as well. Her knees struggled but managed to get her on her feet.

"If I had called you or texted you or emailed you like I so badly wanted to..." he said. He said, "...Well, because of my position here, if you didn't feel the same, if you didn't want to hear from me, that could be constituted as harassment, as me trying to pressure you. The last thing I want is for you to feel pressured. But you should know that I have never stared at my phone waiting for a phone call that wasn't a business deal the way I stared at my phone this entire weekend. The amount of people I wanted to tell to fuck off just for calling and texting while not being you... I've never been so out of sorts in my life."

She looked at him, disbelieving. Unbelieving. Hoping some fantasy of hers had come true. Thinking she would wake up still at her desk with her face in her hands. She actually pinched herself. It didn't break her from this reality, but it brought her out of her daze.

"I'm not used to hearing you swear." This was what she said. If she could have reversed her right foot and brought it up and about in a way that made it so she could physically kick herself in the ass, she would have. There were so many things she wanted to say other than focusing on the fact that he had sworn. That he had used the F word. Had said fuck. *Fuck*.

"Fuck. I should have called," she said. Then they were on each other. He walking around his desk. She walking toward him. With their eagerness they met face first, almost butting heads. Had one of their coworkers opened the office door – a door that was closed but unlocked – they might have thought that the two were engaged in some mutual assault. The fervency with which they kissed and pawed and touched and grabbed and groped could be described as one attacking the other, and the other responding in kind.

I missed this, she thought.

"I missed this," he said. And all at once she wasn't sure if this was need or if this was want, but she knew that this was something she couldn't do without. Need and want are hard to differentiate when the thing you desire inspires them both.

The blinds had been drawn down even before she had entered the glassed-in cubicle that was his new-age office. There wasn't a chance that someone could see them from the outside, but the idea that there were still so many people they knew who hadn't a clue standing right outside drove them both to the same exciting place as they hopped back onto this rollercoaster ride that could end no other way than in a crash.

They did. Crash.

His hips, her hips. Crash.

They collided into each other. His body. Hers...

They had weathered what had been necessary in order to get to this point, crashing and rubbing and attacking one another. Her on top of the desk, him on top of her. They came. Then came the peace of post-passion.

There had been a storm before, perhaps the storm would return after. But in the meanwhile, right then, they were happy where they were, not realizing they were within the eye of that storm.

Other natural disasters apply.

ix.

There they were, Tybalt and Bethany, making one out of two whenever they could find the opportunity. Crashing into each other everywhere.

The bathroom was a frequent spot. Not just either of the bathrooms on their office floor, but also the one in the lobby, those on other floors, the bathroom of a restaurant down the street. Bathrooms in general.

There they were in his office, on the desk with the blinds of his glass enclosure drawn up, exposing their interwovenness whenever they were certain they were the only people on the sales floor. The risk of it all made something that she already considered to be the best ever somehow even better.

Tybalt and Bethany intertwined wherever and whenever they could find a moment alone, and sometimes they didn't necessarily have to be completely alone. Movie theatres were a place they enjoyed, though neither of them was particularly big on movies. Nor did they remember much about the films they attended together. What they did remember was her leaning over and him closing his eyes for several minutes at a time. What they remembered very vividly was his instructing her to come to these movies only in skirts. Short ones.

When the sparse audience in the theatre in which they occupied the back row was particularly engrossed in a fight scene or love scene or chase scene, she would simply sit on her lover's lap and inch her skirt up her hips. And just like that, the movie became far more enjoyable.

They would sneak into those movies in the daytime, a town away or a town after that, or a town away in another direction. Kent, SeaTac, Tacoma, all over King County they crashed and intertwined and interwove and became closer.

Bathrooms, movie theatres, alleyways, wooded areas, cars. Everywhere, they became closer. Physically.

And Bethany began to grow concerned that what they had was only physical and nothing more. She was scared to ask the question. The question that isn't just a question so much as it is an ultimatum no matter how it is worded.

What are we?
Or its other iterations:
Where is this going?
Are we together?
Does this mean anything to you?
Is this just a fling?
They all boil down to one thing, and that is: *if you don't give me the correct answer, we can't continue on this way.*

She knew that if she asked, she would risk losing out on all the fun. She wasn't sure if she could give up the fun... or the hope that this could be something more than just that. Because if she asked, the answer might murder her hope. She wrestled with the idea of hanging on to that hope at the risk of living an illusion. Living an illusion that, if broken, would reveal she was simply just another woman being used for her body.

That went against her values. She wasn't against promiscuity for either of the sexes, but she vowed she wouldn't allow herself to be one of those sappy, sad women who love – yes, that was the only word she could think of to describe how she had come to feel about Mr. Ward during this tsunami of an affair – a man and continue to hang on to him knowing that she wasn't loved back. Bethany had too much pride for that. She had made that mistake once, and she wasn't the type to make the same mistake more than that number.

She had wanted to ask the question as early as a few weeks in, but had decided to give it time. She let the sneaking around and the sex in every and any place that two bodies could fit in continue. She enjoyed it, but the shine of the whole thing was dulled by that question. It continued to snake its way all over and around her brain, wrapping itself around each node, influencing the inhibitors, dampening the dopamine, making it so that everything she thought of was somehow tainted by that question.

What are we?

And its other iterations.

She had let it continue for two months with that question constricting everything that mattered in her head. The pressure became too much as the two were walking out of a noon showing of a movie neither of them would remember watching even a week later.

They were in Tacoma, Washington, on a Saturday. They had both gone to the bathroom after the film, not because they'd had to relieve themselves, but because all four of their hands were sticky and filthy and covered in each other from what they had been doing throughout the showing.

As they got into her car, the words seemed to push themselves out of her without her even realizing she had intended to speak. It was as if she'd thought these thoughts so frequently – had had so many of these thoughts – that there was no longer room for them inside of her mind. They seemed to overflow out of her and began to fill the small space inside the car, threatening to drown the two in the tension that thoughts and words like these often carry.

"I need to know that wanking each other off during daytime horror movies in Tacoma isn't the limit to what we are." Once the words came out of her she had almost laughed at the fact that they hadn't come out in the form of a question after all. Still, she had known it would be an ultimatum. And she had known he would know that.

When he didn't respond for a few moments, she believed that was enough of an answer. Turning the key in the ignition with a shaky hand, she prepared to drop him off at home for the final time. She had put it out there, and now, just as she had feared, the fun was over. *Everything* somehow felt like it was over. Until he made her understand that things hadn't ended, though they would certainly never be the same.

"Stop off at your house first, Betts," Tybalt said. It was said almost in the tone he took at the office, or sometimes during their trysts. It was the tone of Mr. Ward, which meant it was more an order than a request. She had resisted the urge to take her eyes off of the traffic she was merging into in order to look at him.

"Why?" she asked tersely, wanting a response to her statement of an ultimatum, not more orders.

"I figured you'd want to grab a few things so you can stay the night." This time he was all Ty, and not Mr. Ward, her boss, because there was a trace of uncertainty in his voice. She had never spent the night at his place, despite all of the sex they'd had. And, before she could consider what this meant, or even form the words to respond with, Tybalt said,

"There are things you need to know about me before you decide you want to stay in my life, Bethany. These are important things you need to be informed about. Then you can let me know if you want to stick around after that. Because most women wouldn't."

"You can tell me anything, Ty. I hoped you knew that by now."

His response was to reach for the hand that she always kept on the gearshift as she drove, despite the car being automatic. He wove his fingers through hers and left them there as she headed in the direction of her house. This – this hand holding – was something else they had never done until this day. For her, it was both soothing and unnerving.

With a new and unwelcome sense of anxiety in the pit of her stomach, Bethany drove to her place, then his, nearly in complete silence. The entire while she wondered what the man beside her could be capable of, and just how his revelation could destroy her.

X.

"You could say I live a double life," Tybalt began, nearly as soon as he had closed the door to his condo behind them. This much was true. He found that the most convincing lies usually stem from honest places. Mantra 32.

"Pardon me?" Bethany said while removing her shoes. She immediately walked to the couch and sat down. He was glad for that. At least she hadn't bolted out of the apartment. Though he wasn't sure if things wouldn't be better, or easier, if he just let her walk away. He was making life more complicated than it had to be, defying Mantra 29:

KISS – Keep It Simple, Stupid.

Yet here he was, about to do the very opposite.

"Do you remember the night at the hotel in Seattle? After the summit?" he asked her.

"What happened that night, again? It's completely slipped my mind." She said this with a great deal of sarcasm and a minimal amount of humor.

"Alright, smartass, calm down." He smiled at her to show he was joking, but she was clearly too anxious to make any other expression than the one of worry which covered her countenance then. He cut to it.

"I mean, do you remember the files piled up on my desk even though it was a Friday night during a weekend where we were all supposed to be relaxing?"

She remembered the files clearly. They had pushed them aside when he'd taken her on the desk during one of those many times they had let their bodies talk that night.

"That was why I couldn't take the bus back with everyone the day after," he added. "That is how most of my nights are. Mr. Johjima recently hired me to take care of some of his affairs outside of the insurance company. It's busy work, and it's not fun, but it pays well and it'll get me where I need to go. But, I've also signed confidentiality agreements in certain cases. All of that means I'll be very busy for quite a while, and if you ask me what I'm doing I won't always be able to tell you."

He stood in his living room, she sat on the plush leather couch across from him looking troubled. Confused. And for the second time he wondered if she would leave.

Then, he noticed her facial features shift slightly, soften, become more thoughtful. He could see her doing what so many people do when they know they are making the wrong decision. It had been what he had done when he'd asked her over instead of ending things after their movie earlier that afternoon when she had brought this whole thing up. She was rationalizing. Convincing herself that things could be salvaged.

"Is it anything criminal?" she finally asked. He knew then that she had found her boundary. She would let him lead her right up to the point of criminality, but anything past that would be too much for her.

"It is, if you count having only one day free to spend with you as a crime." he responded. She didn't laugh. Bethany looked down and began to fiddle nervously with her fingers. He knew he had to reassure her. "I'm kidding. It's all on the level. Mr. Johjima just has a lot of interests and projects upcoming that will be crucial for him... and for me by association. These projects have to be on the hush, seriously. I wish I could be more forthcoming, I swear. But it wouldn't be right, and I've probably already said too much."

She looked up from her fidgeting hands. Her face defined concern, was synonymous for worry.

"What does that mean for us?"

"That really depends on you, Betts. Right now you only see me at work when we can sneak around, or on Saturdays. And I can't promise that will ever get better with the way Johjima has me running around. Are you sure this is something you can deal with?"

She exhaled loudly, and, along with that air, some of her apprehension seemed to leave her.

"It beats not spending time with you at all." The response was automatic. And honest. Several months ago she wouldn't have been able to picture herself having a personal conversation with this man, now she couldn't picture living without him.

He had begun to walk over to the couch, and before he had even rounded the coffee table between them, she had hiked up her skirt the way he liked her to, and was laying down, waiting for him. When he got there, he climbed atop her. And they communicated the way they did best.

xi.

Roughly four combined orgasms later, only one of them was at ease. Tybalt wriggled free of Bethany who had fallen asleep half on him and half beside him. He was thankful for his oversized couch and for how sound of a sleeper she turned out to be.

Still naked, he walked out onto his balcony. Stood out there in his birth clothes admiring the dimming sky, feeling the cool air drying their shared fluids all over his body. He watched the sun fall, and witnessed the sky turn to fire-colored abstract art.

Usually this scene made him feel like he was on top of the world. The breeze on his body, the cityscape beneath him, behind him a woman who he had just fucked halfway comatose. He should have felt better than he did just then. But there was a nagging feeling wriggling inside of him, and its name was Henry Johjima.

Tybalt replayed, again, what he had just told Bethany. With Mr. Henry Johjima's nagging presence in the back of his mind, he wondered if he had said too much, how what he had said could impact his future. And, as he so often did when he pondered the future he had planned for himself, he thought back to when that future had truly started.

Tybalt reflected on what had actually happened to him on the morning after the summit.

Bethany had just left his room, taking a great deal of his energy with her. He'd been tempted to go back to sleep in the bed that still smelled so much like her. But there was a laptop and files and work that needed his attention.

After he had put on his pajama pants and sat at the desk, just as he was about to turn on the laptop, there had been a knock on the door. Bethany, he had thought to himself. And while he was annoyed with her persistence, he couldn't help but smile at the idea of her. He was trying very hard not to smile when he opened the door. Said,

"I thought we agr–" The words were stopped by the lump which had rapidly developed in his throat when he recognized who was outside of his door. "Mr. Johjima?" Tybalt said in a voice above a whisper, the name barely sneaking its way past that lump in his throat.

He was looking at the owner of the company he worked for, his boss who was dressed very boss-like, standing outside of his hotel bedroom. Tybalt became painfully aware that he was still half naked. Half naked in front of the man he had grown to idolize.

There was a large man with slicked back dark hair dressed in a black blazer standing on the other side of the hall behind Mr. Johjima. Security, Tybalt assumed. He didn't like the looks of any of this.

"I did not mean to disturb you, Mr. Ward."

"No, no, its no disturbance at all. I was just about to get working on some files." He gestured to the open laptop and folders on the table, thankful the desk was in view from the doorway. Mr. Johjima looked surprised.

"Here? On a Saturday?"

"Don't put off until tomorrow what can be done today." Mantra 14. "That's something I live by."

"I see, I see... Well, I am going to have to insist that we put the files off for at least this morning."

Tybalt had looked once again at the large security guard standing behind Mr. Johjima. His face gave away nothing.

"Is there a problem, sir?" Tybalt had asked his boss, thinking about Bethany, knowing that he'd broken the unwritten rules. And not for the first time.

"No problem at all. I would just like to have a discussion with you. I will wait for you to get dressed, then we shall be heading to the conference room."

In fewer than ten minutes Tybalt found himself in the conference room on the second floor of the hotel. He had gotten dressed in his customary suit and tie and was standing across from Mr. Johjima and two others. A boardroom table that took up the majority of the space in the room separated him from them. The large security guard stood behind Tybalt, next to the room's main exit.

"This is Elareen," Mr. Johjima had said as he gestured toward the woman to his left.

Tybalt had looked at the woman. He hadn't been sure whether to walk to the other side of the conference table and shake her hand or stand there and wave. He had settled for a curt nod and said, in words that seemed disconnected from his brain,

"It's nice to meet you."

She had nodded as well but included no words to her greeting.

Exotic. That was the first word that had flashed through Tybalt's head when he had looked at the woman named Elareen. She looked like a woman who could have been from any place. Like a woman who had been many places. She wore dark grey khaki pants and a long-sleeved black sweater. A large white and gray scarf covered her shoulders and half of her torso.

Elareen had olive skin and green eyes that seemed to gleam at Tybalt even across the space created between them by the ten-foot table in the middle of the room. She had black hair pulled back in a ponytail above cutting facial features. Her face was all sharp points and sleek edges, and she was beautiful in the way a sword can be beautiful. In a sense that makes it clear that, if she were touched the wrong way, she could potentially be dangerous.

"And this is Raynaud Bedard." Mr. Johjima had gestured to the man to his right, a short, curly-haired, lightly bearded, middle-aged white man wearing a gray leather jacket, white shirt and blue jeans. "These are my silent partners in many ventures. We are here to offer you an opportunity," Mr. Johjima had stated. He sat. Raynaud sat as well, but Elareen remained standing. When Mr. Johjima motioned for Tybalt to sit across from them, he did as he was bid.

"I'd just like to say," Tybalt began, "thank you for the opportunity to even be given an opportunity. I'm very grateful for your time this morning, Mr. Johjima." Tybalt felt a bit sick after the words left him. His voice still seemed dissociated from his brain. This time it sounded as though it belonged to a snivelling sycophant. Elareen must have heard this too, because she fidgeted where she stood, not bothering to disguise the look of uncertainty she shot toward Mr. Johjima. Raynaud sat there, reclined in his seat, his face much harder to read. Tybalt didn't have to try reading Mr. Johjima's face, his employer's next words confirmed what he had already feared.

"Do not pander." Mr. Johjima stated. "We did not bring you here for that."

"I'm sorry..."

"Do not apologize."

Tybalt kicked himself immediately. He had just gone against the advice of one of the Mantras. Number 16:

Never apologize unless not apologizing costs you something.

Tybalt sat there silently. He felt as though all of the heat in his body had risen to his face. For one of the few times in his life he was thankful for his dark complexion. Thankful that they couldn't see his obvious embarrassment.

He sat up tall in his seat, folded his hands in front of him on the table, and waited. The picture of calm despite his racing nerves. Mantra 19:

Maintain your composure and posture, always.

"We brought you here because of your reputation, Mr. Ward. We sincerely hope that reputation is not all that you are."

Tybalt cleared his throat, found that he was back in association with his voice.

"I suppose we'll have to find out once you tell me what this opportunity of yours is." he said confidently. Henry Johjima had smiled.

"There's the man who turned our Daphnis office around. I enjoyed hearing of your progress as much as I enjoyed our conversation at the summit last night. You have made quite an impression."

"Thank you, sir." Tybalt responded, hoping that 'thank you' wasn't on Mr. Johjima's list of things not to say. Neither Mr. Johjima nor Elareen seemed to be offended. Raynaud still looked stoic. Mr. Johjima continued,

"What I... what we are offering you here is not so much a promotion as it is an increase in status. My associates and I work for a special... branch under the Helping Hand tree. An organization called The Fold."

Tybalt scanned his memory. He knew Henry Johjima owned many other companies and undertook other endeavors outside of Insurance. Tybalt knew of the man's stake in a major west coast movie production company, knew of Helping Hand Publishing House, the slew of charitable and philanthropic projects the aging Asian businessman dealt with, including the chain of Foster's Family Restaurants he owned around North America. He had read up on the man intently, wanting to emulate him. Yet he had never heard of The Fold. Tybalt was perplexed. Upset with himself for not knowing of this vital piece of knowledge. What if Mr. Johjima had questions for him?

Overprepare so you are always prepared – Mantra 15 was one he reminded himself of hourly.

"You see that look on Mr. Ward's face, Raynaud? This is why he is here. Do you know why I like that look on this man's face?"

"Why do you like that look, Johjima?" Raynaud answered, speaking for the first time. His accent was obviously French, his tone was much more difficult to interpret. He almost seemed disinterested. Tybalt did his best to set his face back to neutral despite Mr. Johjima's words.

"That was the expression of a man who expected to know, and who was displeased with not knowing because he has done his homework very thoroughly. You are right to be confused, Mr. Ward. If you had known what I was referring to, I would be disappointed in myself." Mr. Johjima chuckled. Both Raynaud and Elareen remained stone-faced. "The Fold is more of a... covert organization."

"Covert as in..." Tybalt had nearly said the word 'spies' to complete that sentence, but immediately felt it would be in his best interest to allow his employer to fill in the blank.

"As in, only those who need to know need to know. And those who do not need to know need never find out. What we need to find out, right now, is whether or not you need to know, Mr. Ward. What do you think? Do you?"

"You don't ask questions you aren't fairly certain of the answers to, Mr. Johjima. That much of the homework I've done on you I'm confident about. If I didn't need to know, you wouldn't have let me know there was something that needed knowing." Tybalt answered without skipping a beat. Mr. Johjima chuckled again, and this time Raynaud broke into a smile. He nodded approvingly at Tybalt.

Elareen still looked as though she might lacerate anything that attempted to handle her the wrong way, or attempted to handle her at all.

Two out of three ain't bad, *Tybalt thought as he returned the smiles of the two men in the room.*

"Well done, Mr. Ward. We have one year to find out if you truly need to know. Standard probationary period. During said time we will have one main assignment for you. If you meet your targets, you will get to know. If you do not meet your targets, our association will come to an end and this very conversation will become a figment of your imagination. I would ask you if you are still interested but you are correct, I already know the answer. There will be some perks, probationary benefits let us call them. A car service will be made available to you twenty-four hours of the day. Women will be provided to you as you require. Life will be made slightly easier so that you will be able to fully focus on your goals. All we ask, essentially, is that you continue to do what you do best: persuade and convince." When Mr. Johjima had mentioned the women, Tybalt had looked at Elareen to gauge her reaction. Elareen's eyes were jade daggers. She tilted her head slightly, as if to ask Tybalt what it was he was looking for that may have been in her direction.

Tybalt wondered if he was still in his hotel room, in his bed which would still have been slightly damp from he and Bethany, dreaming all of this. The longer it went on, the less real it felt.

"Why me? Why now?"

"We are aware of your history, Mr. Ward." For a heart stopping moment Tybalt believed his boss was talking about his father. The shame his father had brought to Tybalt's family after he'd died. During his life. The shame Tybalt had worked so hard to separate himself from, to keep buried in the past. It was moments like this that he wished what he'd told Bethany about his father on the bus were true. He was relieved when Mr. Johjima continued speaking, *"We know of your proclivities and are aware of your lifestyle. We have been told for the better part of a year of your ability to be as ruthless as you are charming, as unbending as you are persuasive. Why you, Mr. Ward? Because you are who you*

are. Why now? Seeing you in action yesterday, your speech, your interactions, it all made me aware that we had already wasted too much time. You are a special sort of salesman, Mr. Ward."

"I appreciate the kind words, Mr. Johjima. But I get the feeling you didn't research me, bring me to this unscheduled meeting and cause me to miss the bus back to Daphnis just to encourage me to keep up the great insurance sales. I don't think we're talking insurance here at all. What is it exactly that I will be selling for you?" Again, he thought of his father.

"Ah, there it is. I appreciate a man who cuts to the core of things. What we need for you to sell is a lifestyle. The hope of a lifestyle. There are certain types of people you may have access to who we are very interested in. What we want from you is to make them interested in us. What we want, Mr. Ward, is for you to help us groom them for this lifestyle..."

Tybalt was jolted from his reverie when he felt arms wrap around his naked waist. He wasn't sure how long he had been out there on the balcony reflecting. Calculating and recalculating; Mantras 3 and 4 taking over his mind.

"I don't think I've ever seen you so lost in thought," Bethany, the owner of the arms which had wrapped around him, whispered in his ear. "Didn't you hear me open the balcony door?"

"I did." He hadn't. "But I do have a lot on my mind."

"I didn't mean to freak you out, you know... with what I asked you earlier. It's just that I don't like my time wasted any more than you do."

He turned in her arms, to look at her. She had him pinned against the railing, only glass and steel separating them from gravity's deadly pull.

"I'm not freaked out, I'm just figuring out the risk." She wondered if he was making an insurance joke, but his face was set to stern. Focused. "We have to not just make it work here, but we have to make it work at work. Which means being careful. Which means this has to stay a secret. Is that okay with you, Betts? I want you to *really* think about that."

She didn't give it much thought at all.

"You actually believe I want everyone to know I'm sleeping with my boss?" They both laughed at this, until she looked at him sincerely. "Do you think we can actually make this work?"

"Yes." He calculated. "If we plan things out just right, we'll all get exactly what we want."

xii.

It was that moment, the moment when they had stood naked on the balcony lying to themselves, that was the apex, the crescendo, the zenith. For Bethany, it was the heighth of happiness.

The inevitable next step was the downhill portion of things.

It didn't happen immediately; rather, it was a ride down a gentle slope. A slow gradient that allowed one to believe that a plunge downhill wasn't in the offing.

In Bethany's mind, they had made progress. They'd begun dating, not just screwing. There was still the sneaking around due to the nature of their relationship and the conflict that would arise if they were discovered, but now they went to restaurants, and not just to make use of their bathrooms. They would go to movies to watch them, and actually discuss the films afterward. She would stay over every Saturday, but was always asked to leave promptly on Sunday morning at 8 AM. Tybalt let her know that Sunday was his one day to relax. The one day that he ignored all things work and world, choosing to focus on himself.

He told her about his Sunday morning meditation, his sometimes hours-long bath, his run. The fact that he took the Sunday to really clean up the house, and that it was this cleaning process which gave him a release, a sense of renewal.

She loved the idea of it all, and told him that she would consider doing the same for herself on Sundays. They could reset at the same time, even if they did so separately. He encouraged her a great deal. Said it was a wonderful way to really release the tensions.

The first Sunday she had tried it she believed him to be a genius. She had struggled with meditating for more than five minutes, though the rest went smoothly. She went for a run, took a long bath, went to a masseuse at a spa that was so good she purchased two gift certificates – one for herself, one for Tybalt – for an upcoming Sunday at the establishment.

Their relationship began to truly gain its momentum downhill the moment the cashier said, 'Have a nice day' and placed those certificates in Bethany's hand. She had smiled and said, 'Thank you', not realizing how a pair of gift certificates could so thoroughly ruin one's life.

xiii.

She had surprised him with his spa certificate the following Saturday. And, for some reason she would never understand, she had brought both certificates with her. Perhaps it was a subliminal thing. Maybe she had thought on some level that, if he saw the certificates together, he might suggest going together. This would have been wishful thinking, even on the subconscious level.

He had been grateful for his gift. So grateful that he'd put the two certificates together on the coffee table in his living room before immediately carrying her into his bedroom.

Bethany left a few minutes before 8 AM the following Sunday morning as always. It wasn't until several hours later, when she was about to walk into the spa to begin her day of releasing tension, that she realized she'd forgotten her certificate at Tybalt's place. Annoyed, but secretly excited that she could potentially get to see her man one more time that day, she looked at her watch. She did some calculating of her own, and determined that she could get to his place and back in time to make her appointment. That's what she aimed to do.

She had parked illegally when she got to Mr. Ward's building. Raced inside. The guard on duty buzzed her in, recognizing that she was Mr. Ward's special lady friend from the night before. From many Saturday nights prior to that.

She elevated to the eighteenth floor, sped to his apartment door. She went to knock but decided to reach for the doorknob instead. To let herself in. There was no point having him get out of his bath or snap out of his meditative state just to open the door for her. Besides, she was looking forward to surprising him with a kiss before she grabbed her certificate and fled to her appointment. She hoped he wouldn't be angry about her brief intrusion into his day of release.

The door wasn't locked. She was thankful for this even while she wondered if he actually liked surprises. She was both excited and nervous about finding out. Bethany grinned like a ninny as she considered all of the information they had yet to learn about each other. She was thinking that their honeymoon phase could be greatly extended based on this alone as she walked into the apartment.

The living room was empty. She had hoped to find him there.

"Probably in the bathtub," Beth whispered out loud to herself. She made a brief detour to the living room to grab her spa certificate before heading down the hallway that led to his bedroom.

She heard a clapping sound as she entered further into the apartment.

Loud. Rhythmic. Repetitive. It sounded like applause.

The sound stole into her head in an unsettling way that she didn't quite understand. She let it go. Continued smiling, continued walking deeper into his home. Knowing him, she told herself, he was probably watching a Ted Talk in his bedroom and clapping at the end along with the audience. The guy never stopped looking for ways to motivate himself. She was starting to envy that.

The loud applause continued, slightly muffled by the closed bedroom door. She opened the door, walked into the room mouth first, her lips already puckered as she prepared to surprise her man with a kiss. Then those puckered lips had parted to become an 'O'. The sound she had been hearing at once making sense.

Clap! Clap! Clap! Clap!
Clapclapclapclapclapclapclap! Etcetera.

The smell hit her a moment after the sound registered. It was the smell of effort, exertion. It was the smell of bodies. Betrayal.

She had walked in on something that was supposed to be sex but looked like violent pleasure. Or maybe just violence.

It was like nothing she'd had with him, not with the way he was almost lunging into the woman bent over on the bed in front of him. Tybalt was mauling her, treating her like he hated her, or perhaps was indifferent to her. It was a level of savagery she wouldn't have thought he was capable of. For a moment, she put her jealousy and anger aside to wonder if she should call for help.

But then she noticed the ball gag.

She noticed the nipple clamps.

The clothespins pinching the young Asian woman's breasts, threatening to break the skin. There were blotches of pink and red all over the woman's chest. She saw all of that and knew that this was their thing – her man and his mistress. Sex and violence was theirs, just as sex and sneaking around had been Bethany's and his. She was his outlet on Saturdays, this was his outlet on Sundays. And God only knew what really went on during the rest of the week.

Apparently, he was a man that required plenty of release because she had made love to him just hours before walking in on this scene. Bethany usually wasn't the type of person to use the term 'making love', though now, watching what sex looked like between him and this strange woman who appeared to be wearing a maid's outfit, she understood that what they had done was different than whatever this was. Vastly.

This wasn't so much sex as it was dominance. Tybalt Ward, the dominator, the tyrant she'd always known him to be before that stupid bus ride had changed her mind.

Bethany felt ill, felt sickness creeping upward.

She wasn't going to say anything. She was going to back away slowly, leave. Then came the second betrayal inside the last few minutes, this one by her own knees as they buckled, ruining her plans to sneak away by bringing her off balance. She'd had to grab onto his doorway to keep herself from falling completely. In her attempts to not fall over, her body had hit the partially ajar door, causing it to swing open, hitting the wall behind it. The noise caused the two who were engaged in carnal violence to turn their attention to her.

There was a **clap** or two more before they stilled and all sound (except for that of heavy breathing) left the room.

The woman was still on her hands and knees, Tybalt was still behind her. They both stared at Bethany, each of them stunned into motionlessness.

"I came for my spa certificate..." She held the certificate up for the two to see, as though she had to prove her explanation. "I... I left it here by accident I'm sor..." she caught herself just as she nearly apologized to him.

She had been about to apologize to *him*.

This was the part of the entire ordeal that had made her angrier than anything else. He had snowed her over so thoroughly that, even when he was doing the worst of things, she couldn't see him for what he was. Didn't want to. Because that would mean he had been exactly who she had thought he was after years of working together. The person she thought he was before the bus ride and the breathing. Before the talking. It would mean he truly was rigid and mean and cold and heartless. This was the same man whose entire outlook on life centered around surviving while others fell to the wayside. She had allowed herself to be talked into believing that the cold character he became at work was a persona he put on, in the same way he put on the fancy clothes and shoes to match it. He had convinced her that he put on that persona for the big shots like Mr. Johjima and the other higher-ups. She was now starting to wonder if the hardcase he was at work was the true him, and if the sweet, kind, caring, loving, tender person she had spent so much time with over the last several months was the persona he put on just for her sake. Always Mr. Ward and never truly the man she had come to know simply as Ty.

If she hadn't been sure which was the real version of him when she'd walked in and seen what she had seen, she was made certain by his next words, spoken to the young lady who he had exited after Bethany had interrupted them. He grabbed one of his bedsheets and wrapped himself in it. Then, to the dark-haired young woman in the maid's uniform, he said,

"To the closet. Go."

Bethany watched in muted disbelief as the young woman crawled down from the bed and crawled across the hardwood floor of Tybalt's bedroom. She approached the closet, got to her knees, opened it and then crawled in, quietly sliding the door closed behind her, but not before making eye contact with Bethany. She saw fear there, in the younger woman's deep, dark eyes. But there was also something else that Bethany saw, something that glimmered like excitement. Betts wasn't sure whether she wanted to save the girl or run over there and rip her face off, glimmering eyes included. Especially.

"Ty..."

"Betts." He hadn't made a move to step toward her. Neither of them seemed to want to move. They were teetering here, between the beauty of what they'd had and the abyss that would be their future, and neither of them were eager to fall into that darkness. "I told you that you couldn't be here on Sundays."

"I forgot my massage certfic– That's not the fucking point! That's the *last* thing that should matter. How could you do this to me?"

"What is it that I've done to you, exactly?" He stood there with an expression on his face that was no expression at all. His hands were at his hips, holding up his bedsheet toga. His muscles rippled with their previous exertion, the skin atop them glistened with sweat. It further infuriated her that he somehow still looked stately. Pompous. *Good.*

She looked at him, her mouth agape, her head swiveling back and forth between his smug and remorseless face and the closed closet door, behind which was a young Asian woman in a kinky maid's outfit with nipple clamps and clothespins all over her breasts, and a ball gag in her mouth.

"Do I really have to *say* it? Holy shit, Ty, you were just fucking some whore who crawled into your closet on command!"

"Please don't shout. And yes, I know what happened. But, Betts, you don't own me and I don't own you. I've never told you that you couldn't be with anyone else." The words reached from his mouth to her face, slapping her with their truth. He had told her they'd graduated from the level of fooling around on Saturday afternoons at the Regal South Hill Cinema 6 in Puyallup, and she had launched herself to the conclusion of exclusivity.

Of girlfriend and boyfriend.

Not this.

"This..." he'd nodded to the closet. "...is just physical. She comes here, helps me clean the place and then gives me a release that only girls like her can give."

"Girls *like* her?" Bethany let these words sink in. *Girls like her...* "Oh my God. We stopped using condoms! Are you not using condoms with her either?" She looked down at his crotch, but it was covered by the bedspread. He was still hard, and the sight of his obvious excitement even in the middle of all of this repulsed her. She tried to remember if she had seen a condom on him when he'd pulled out of the girl who she was now thinking of as the hooker in the closet. "If you've given me some kind of disease, I swear to God—"

"She's clean. We have her tested monthly."

"Oh God. I don't even want to know what the fuck that means!"

"Betts... Bethany. We can make this work. We make a great team, here and at the office. But we can't get so caught up caring about the physical stuff. We're people, not possessions. You and I fit together on so many levels." He took steps toward her, and for a brief moment she almost let him get close enough to touch her hand.

If he had touched her hand, she knew she would have forgiven him. Or, more accurately, accepted whatever this was. She would have been letting him touch her with hands that had just been on and inside of the whore wearing a maid's uniform who was in the closet a few yards from Bethany, and she would somehow find a way to convince herself that it was okay. She couldn't let that happen. She couldn't let him touch her and put her deeper under his spell.

Bethany bolted.

As she made her way down the hallway, she thought she heard him telling her to take her things with her. She didn't go back for clarification, or for her things.

She had run until she was out of the apartment, down the seventeen flights of stairs, out of the building and at her car. She jumped in, out of breath, forced herself to not cry, and drove – perhaps a little too quickly – to the only place that she knew to go. To the only person she could think of that might be able to help her make sense of this. Or at least help her feel like she could get over this betrayal.

She had driven to Reese Mitchell's house, her favorite co-worker. Her best friend.

He had answered the door to her frenzied knocking.

They spoke for a brief period. A brief period that would stretch into forever for Bethany.

A few hours after she had left Reese's home, the young man was found dead.

SHE RAGED

ii.

"You want me to read you the last thing he emailed me? You want to hear the last thing he wanted me to know?" Bethany's voice was fracturing, threatening to break. She had been raging for minutes by this point. Speaking in a tone and at a decibel level entirely inappropriate for an office environment. She had screamed many things since she'd started in on Mr. Ward. What she hadn't screamed, hadn't said aloud, was the reason she believed Reese had sent her an email. She didn't say that he had tried to call her after she had left his place, or that she had been too upset to answer. To call back. Too upset to respond to Reese's texts. That truth was too painful to admit. Those words stayed inside of her, cutting her internally.

This was roughly a month after Reese Mitchell had been found dead, evidently a victim of suicide. This was where we started and where we left off, with Bethany Helmsley raging at her boss and ex-lover, Mr. Tybalt Ward.

She had just come back to work after mourning Reese, hoping that she could look past the fact that she had allowed Tybalt to con her – had given him so much of herself – and still work in the same space he occupied. But the line he had just crossed, the line between him being just another sex-hungry man corrupted by power and him being a truly evil human being, was one he could not come back from.

He had mocked Reese's death, and that was something Bethany wouldn't allow him to get away with.

She looked at him before continuing to search her phone for the suicide note that Reese had left her. She wanted to read it in an attempt to make him feel bad, feel empathetic, feel sympathetic. Feel something. But even as she prepared herself to read, she knew her plan (if it could be called that) was futile. Whichever Ty she had fallen in love with was not the one in front of her. That Ty didn't exist. Never had. He was a construct of this monster.

Ty the Terrible. Ty for Tyrant.

"I always thought I understood, but I guess I didn't." Bethany spoke to Mr. Ward, to their audience around the office, as she clicked and pressed and swiped on her phone with trembling hands. "I guess he knew I didn't. And that's what I'll have to live with for the rest of my fucking life. Because people like you, and maybe even me, maybe... People like you don't even bother to try to fucking understand, because it's too hard for you. But maybe if you hear this you'll know. You'll fucking get it." She stopped her speech, her focus on the screen in her hands, her lips still moving. She was reading something now, and when she got to a certain point on the screen her eyes lit up. A pair of sparklers burning in her skull. Bethany looked, to Tybalt, like a scientist, long since gone mad, rediscovering the hypothesis which had driven her there in the first place. Her lips were dry, her eyes bloodshot, her hair frazzled and frayed. She looked, to Tybalt, like poor mental health.

"Here!" she said abruptly, finding what she had been scrolling for. "Here! Here!" Her voice was frantic. It warped and warbled, as if both a sob and a laugh were fighting to come out of her throat at the same time. "Here's what he said: '...It's like a gnat's inside your head... an evil gnat that wants you dead. It digs around and finds your weaknesses and your worries. All of the doubts you've worked your whole life to overcome, it unburies. It spreads those doubts everywhere. All over your confidence. It crawls around your brain, drawing out your every insecurity, your every piece of self-loathing, your every single recollection of each time you'd felt as though you'd made a fool of yourself, or had been embarrassed, or had fucked up and been ashamed. It somehow gets these once diminished memories to grow and breathe and feel real again, just as painfully as when the memories were fresh. These thoughts just become too much to deal with…'" She stopped, scanned down the screen with her eyes. Continued, "'…It's like your very worst enemy lives inside of your head, and not only does he know how to find all of your weaknesses, but he knows how to use them all against you. He knows exactly how to torture you. Ask anyone who has been tortured, physically or psychologically, it's only a matter of time until you'd just prefer death. That's what my brain feels like and I'm tired of it, Betts. I'm tired. I love you, but I hate this gnat even more, and you know how much I love you. Please don't be mad at you. I'm not.'"

By the end of all of this she may as well have been reading the suicide note with her face pressed inside of a shallow puddle. She bubbled and burbled the words from inside a cascade of tears.

Tybalt didn't respond well to tears, or so he'd been told. There had been a time when he had responded well. Appropriately, at least. A time where he had said 'there, there' and 'I'm here for you' and 'it'll be okay'.

Hugged them.

Held them.

Forgave them.

It was early on in his love life, early enough so that he did not know the rules of love, relationships and courtship. Didn't know, in fact, that these things came with rules. But they did. And it wasn't until he realized how often he'd been made to be a loser, a sucker, that he even knew he was playing a game. It was the tears that had done it. The realization that he had, for so long, been duped by so many women who had shed so many tears caused him to vow he would never be manipulated in that way ever again.

He had willed himself to become averse to tears over the years. They were a sign of being too much of a coward to face things head on. Another sign of weakness. For weakness, Tybalt had no room in his life.

So, while Bethany's tears and tales of her friend were meant to reach Tybalt, to appeal to some more sympathetic inner him, they only acted as a trigger for his disdain. His disdain often led to mockery. Mockery fueled by memories of women from relationships past who had lied and cried and caused both sympathy and empathy within Tybalt to die. It was that tear-inspired disdain that caused him to reply,

"I'm surprised he didn't do it sooner," followed by a sound that Bethany considered to be close enough to a laugh that it caused her to begin to truly lose it. Her mind, many rational portions of it, was currently escaping her.

"How can you say such a fucking thing?" Her hands flew down to her sides, her arms becoming rigid as she began to make an odd marching-on-the-spot movement. Tybalt was reminded of a bull about to charge.

She was now in the middle of truly losing it.

"Look. All I'm saying is that he wasn't enjoying life. Wasn't making the best of it. He made a choice. Why am I such a bad guy for respecting the choice he made and moving on?"

"You just don't fucking get it."

"Oh, I think I got it pretty good, don't you?" His voice was peppered with innuendo. She felt revolted.

"Go fuck yourself."

"Oh Betts, we both know I don't ever have to do *that*." Again, he made a sound that came close to laughter, and that is when Bethany finally lost it. Truly.

There are moments, an unfortunate some can tell you, when you can see the light evacuating what was once an illuminated soul, leaving behind only darkness, only an unseeing, hungry need for a satisfaction that almost always borders upon the abominable.

This was the moment the Last Light left Bethany Helmsley.

Her face screwed up until it was nearly unrecognizable. Gasps could be heard. Lowly. A few of those in the room took steps backward. One young woman turned and walked quickly away, apparently all at once becoming allergic to confrontation. They reacted this way because they saw what she was about to do.

Bethany – Betts to Reese Mitchell – cocked back her arm and hurled her phone at her manager, Fuck Buddy, Dominator.

She immediately regretted the decision.

He moved his head to the left, not that he needed to, the phone had missed by a mile or so. It hit the large window a few feet behind him and it shattered – the phone, not the window – falling to the floor and immediately becoming refuse.

For a terrifying moment, Betts seriously considered following the phone's path and seeing if she could shatter the high rise's window, maybe with the combination of her weight as well as Tybalt's. Though she would have preferred better company on the way down.

She controlled herself. Barely. The gnat wasn't in her head, she told herself. She was just being emotional. This wasn't what Reese would have wanted.

She turned.

She headed toward the exit, not sure how or if she would be able to come back the next day, or again.

She didn't have to wonder for long before she found out.

His voice whiplashed into the air, a Cat O' Nine Tails lashing at her head and brain and ears and the drums inside them.

"Take your things with you." And, unlike the day of the gift certificate, this time she was certain he had said the words.

She half turned, looked at him from one wet and reddened eye, pondering physical violence once again. Instead, she whispered something vulgar under her breath just before she bit her tongue. She had said enough. She had had enough.

Bethany walked away, leaving her belongings, her coworkers, her entire life behind. She took nothing, not wanting to give him the satisfaction of watching her pack up her things.

SILENCE

It was one week after Bethany had walked away from her desk without her things. She was currently on her couch, in her pajamas, at mid-day, contemplating what she wanted out of life. Considering the things she truly cared about.

She had missed five business days, had no more sick days, couldn't tap into short term or long-term disability. She wasn't even certain she still had a job, but she didn't care about any of that.

She did care about having enough money to get herself a sufficient amount of wine. A quantity of cheap vino that would make it so she wouldn't have to go back to sobriety other than during the foggy first few minutes after waking up from each blackout (what she did these days couldn't quite be called sleeping).

What she cared about was having enough money to buy a quantity of marijuana that would make it so she wouldn't have to touch the ground for a while. For the rest of her life, she wished.

What she cared about was having the sort of money in her bank account that would afford her the chance to buy the fentanyl patches her guy – an old friend from Washington State University – had promised her he could keep supplying her with.

Right now, she had all of those things. In her, all at once.

She had chewed on one of them, a Fentanyl patch. Something she was told was referred to as Jackpot. She quickly understood why. Then she had smoked a wonderful Indica called Pink Rockstar. Drunk cheap Californian wine before she proceeded to chew again, smoke again, continued drinking until she became a human puddle on her couch. She was doing what her little brother would have called 'zoning the fuck out'. And, for the first time in all the years since she had quit doing the hard stuff, in all the time she had spent nagging her brother, trying to reason with him and trying to get him to get himself to want to get clean, she understood why he wouldn't.

This just felt so much better than real life.

This was the most relaxed she had ever been. *Meditation's got nothing on this*. She wanted to laugh at that thought, but her face was too relaxed to do the work, so she only lay there, slumped. Her eyes were half-lidded, her pupils seemed to register everything through a thin film of I-don't-give-a-fuck-about-what-I'm-seeing.

Because this felt far better than focusing on stuff.

She was zoning. In and (the fuck) out. Registering then forgetting then remembering that she was watching an old episode of *Friends*. *The One With The Proposal: Part 2*. The one where Rachel and Phoebe needed a backup husband, a 'Just in case I'm not married by this age, will you marry me?'. Someone who would say yes to that question.

Bethany was reminded that she and Reese had once made a pact to be one another's backup spousal options. A thousand years ago. In another lifetime. In another dimension. Maybe one where he could still be alive.

They had laughed, drunk wine, and said that they were the Phoebe and Joey of the bunch, with her being Joey. They'd laughed at that too. So much.

It hurt her to think about it, a hurt she felt despite the opioids and the marijuana and the booze. It was a pain that powerful.

She topped up.

Gulped.

Topped up.

What happened next was what had been happening since she had found out, by seeing a Facebook post, that Reese had died. What happened next was that any memory of him led her to the last memory of the two of them together, and how she had raged.

But first she had wept.

Bethany had refused to cry in front of Tybalt before speeding away from his home on that fateful Sunday afternoon. She had turned to Reese instead. He was one of the few people alive (at the time) she had felt comfortable crying to.

She had gone to him at his house. Reese was rarely elsewhere on a Sunday, and she knew she had an open invite. She'd headed there seeking out her best friend to tell him everything about her and their boss. To come clean. To attain a bit of catharsis.

This had been the biggest secret she had ever kept from him during their friendship, the only secret. And now that it had blown up in her face, she saw no reason to keep it secret any longer. She knew he would understand why she had felt the need to keep it from him.

He'd had secrets too.

Bethany now recalled it all in the hazy sort of way she thought of things when she was in a wooze. Zoning. The memories coming at her as photographs, still-shots. The words spoken in those moments affixed themselves to each snapshot of a memory like a page from a picture book.

She remembered getting there, remembered trembling, but couldn't recall whether or not it had been a cold day. She remembered standing there, the tears already streaming down her face as she waited for him to open the door.

There was the image of the look on his face when he had opened the door. When she looked back at this still-shot and rotated it in her mind, zoomed in, inspected, she always remembered clearly that his eyes were red. Though in the actual moment, she hadn't noticed his red eyes at all. If she had, she may have changed the way she had gone about things.

"I've been having an affair with Mr. Ward," she remembered saying to him before any other words were spoken. And his expression wasn't the mask of surprise she'd been expecting. He had looked more disappointed, almost disgusted.

"Half of the women in that building have had an affair with Mr. Ward, Betts." The way he said it may as well have been him winding up and punching her in the gut. Reese had twisted the term 'had an affair' in his mouth, making her choice of words to describe what had gone on between her and her boss sound like a mockery. The addition of her name at the end of his sentence made it sound like an admonishment. The statement was smeared with disapproval.

Oh my God he's judging me. I can't believe he's judging me. I can't handle this right now.

She had thought that then. She thinks this now, in her wooze. Zoning. A photo reel playing in her mind.

"All I'm saying, Betts, is that the guy is a sleazebag. He's not worth you getting this worked up over. Have you been tested?"

And all at once she believed she had made a terrible mistake by going there.

"What?" was all she could say in response. The memory-image was of her face, stunned, flabbergasted.

"It would be smart if you got tested. I'm just sayi–"

"That's the first thing you say to me? That? You think you can stand there and judge me after you traipse around from guy to guy every Friday night like some little whore."

Reese was gay. Reese was promiscuous. For him, Friday nights had been coined as Gay's Night Out. She had laughed at this until he had said she wouldn't ever be invited.

She didn't qualify, that was made clear right in the title of the thing.

Bethany had always known that the real reason she didn't qualify was because she could often be Reese's conscience. And on Fridays he liked to live life without one.

Bethany had viewed Reese's promiscuity as one of the reasons she believed he wouldn't judge her recent actions. She had been devastated to find herself standing there, being judged.

"Betts. Liste–"

"No. You listen. I came here thinking that I would have a friend, but I should have known that was way too much to ask from someone like you." She paused, and when he only stared at her with resignation in his expression, she went on, "You're selfish. You've always been selfish. I'm always here for you and it's always about you, and when I finally come to you with something huge you make me feel like a bug. Like a little pointless fucking insect. I should have known not to come to you with this."

With that, she had turned and left. She had stormed away from his house, not knowing that she was leaving behind the last words she would ever say to her best friend, and that she would never be able to take them back. It wasn't just her words she had left behind, it was Reese himself. And he would subsequently go on to leave her behind in a much more permanent way.

She had tried to convince herself that his actions weren't the result of her own, but she could never truly believe that.

If only she'd noticed that he had been crying before he'd answered the door. Maybe it would all have gone differently.

He'd had secrets too.

His were bigger than hers. His were life altering.

It wasn't until days after Reese's funeral that Bethany had gotten a chance to really speak with Mrs. Heather

Mitchell, Reese's mother. Betts had been going to visit Mrs. Mitchell each night since her only son had quietly died, his life leaking away into a bathtub that had been full of red by the time the door to the bathroom was kicked open. He had been her only son and the only person she'd had in her life.

The two had shared a home. Reese's father had divorced himself from Reese's mother (and him, by association) two decades prior. She had never remarried or even dated, had never gone back to her maiden name. Bethany had felt as though being there for the grieving woman would make up for the way she hadn't been there for her son.

Until this particular night, the older woman had not been up to talking. Previous visits had involved Betts feeding the older woman, soothing her. Betts putting a comedy on the television and hoping that it would make one or both of them laugh even though she knew that neither of them were truly ever watching. But on this particular night, four days after Reese's funeral, Betts had convinced Mrs. Mitchell to have a drink of tea with her in the kitchen, away from the living room that had since become a den of sadness. There had been actual conversation about the young man they had mutually loved. Mrs. Mitchell had started that conversation by accidentally revealing one of Reese's secrets, not imagining that Bethany couldn't have known considering how close the two had been.

"He just didn't want to live with it. I mean, we both knew he could live with it... Medications are a lot better than they were before. In the 80s and 90s, during the epidemics. But I think it was the shame he didn't want to live with as much as the disease itself."

Betts had only nodded, sipping tea that was piping hot but felt ice cold as she swallowed it along with this new piece of information. She had kept her poker face, acting as though she knew what Mrs. Mitchell was talking about.

"We talked about it. That's the frustrating part. We both talked about how advanced the medicine had gotten. Both the medicine and the community. But he didn't want to deal with it; the medication, the going to the doctor all the time, the constant testing and poking and prodding... He was such a big baby when it came to needles... the serosorting, the shame, the 'having to identify as yet another thing that the world was disgusted by'. That's how he put it in the letter he left me. Oh, my baby was so smart... So sad and smart." Then she had broken down. And Bethany would, for the rest of her life, remember the image of that moment, of a rapidly aging woman with her head bowed over a cup of tea, tears falling into and around it. And herself watching that woman. Stunned.

He'd had secrets too.

'Have you been tested?' She remembered the question now. He had asked out of genuine concern because he'd just been diagnosed with HIV. And she had been an absolute asshole about it. Then he killed himself, and a part of her with him.

In her wooze, Bethany wondered if Heath – Reese's office fling – knew, and if she was a terrible person for not bringing it up to her co-worker. *He'll find out eventually... one way or another*, she thought.

She was barely conscious. She heard laughter coming out of her television and, for a moment, forgot why. *People laugh, not TVs*, she thought, before laughing in her mind. But that laughter didn't reach her face.

Then that laughter, even though it was internal, caused her guilt, because it made her think of Reese again. Everything made her think of the second of her two dead best friends.

Again, she replayed her fight with Reese over Mr. Ward, the memory on an endless loop. A never-ending confirmation of her being scum. Mr. Ward was certainly scum, and she had convinced herself to love him. So, what did that make her? *Scum times two,* she thought slowly. Hazily.

"Douba da thumm." Double the scum is what she meant to say, but the words were slurred by all the wine sloshing around in her system, making her feel slow and dim, not quite there, not quite anywhere. The wine and the Jackpot. The wine and the Jackpot and the weed she'd been smoking all evening that had put her into this wooze. It was a wonderful feeling, and she was thankful for it.

She considered reaching out to her brother just then. That was the thought most clear in the haze that had begun to overtake her mind. But why bother? *He always never listens to me anyways so why would he even cares?*

Zoning.

She was nearly laying down, the back of her head and neck on the arm of her couch. She failed in an attempt to shift her body upward so that she could sit and take a sip of the drink that was in her hand, resting on her lap. Her body seemed to be disconnected from her brain.

As she attempted to raise her drink to her lips, her hand trembled just enough for the drink to spill in her lap and pool beneath her. She went to reach for the felled glass, but nothing moved.

She saw the spilled red wine on her gray pajama pants, felt it between her thighs and the couch, and thought of her first period.

She closed her eyes.

Part Two

Suicide

GNATS

i.

Tybalt Ward was nearly in a panic, standing outside of the door to his own condominium unit trying to figure out how to open it using only his feet. He held several shopping bags in his hands – the solution to his problems. He hoped.

He had an infestation, and no one was taking it seriously. Three times he had called the Superintendent, three times the little flies had hidden when the Super had come in for an inspection. The Super had refused to fumigate the building.

Tybalt had then called an independent exterminator, a real well renowned bug guy. A guy he'd been able to get on short notice through his connections with The Fold, through Helping Hand. Even the bug pro had refused the thousands that Tybalt had offered him to get rid of the flies. The gnats.

The exterminator had found a few fruit flies in the kitchen, 'but nothing to warrant an infestation,' he'd said. The bug guy had looked at Tybalt, bug-eyed as he rushed out of the unit, Ty insisting on paying him ten thousand dollars to just do the job and not argue. The exterminator had run away. He had been tempted, but had known that exposing the rest of the tenants in the building to toxic fumes just because this nut job was afraid of a few flies would bring him more trouble than the big pay day was worth.

That had been a week ago.

Ty wondered now how things could go so sideways so quickly. How he could so soon lose the control he had only recently begun to have a taste of.

He thought back to that first meeting with Mr. Johjima and his associates on the day after the summit. He thought about that meeting constantly now.

He had left the hotel conference room that day as a man who could walk on air. He could never have guessed the fall from grace would be so devastating.

The day that Mr. Johjima had informed him of The Fold and their Lifestyle seemed so long ago, so far away, though it hadn't even been a year since that beautiful day.

Everything had been at his fingertips, all that he'd ever wanted just within his reach.

Now, as he stood outside of his apartment, hands full of shopping bags containing what he hoped would be the first step toward rising up again, he wondered how all of it could have slipped so quickly out of his grasp.

He used his foot to manipulate the door handle until he got it open.

With the door slightly ajar, he shouldered it far enough open to squeeze in, then he closed the door behind him and prepared himself...

BEFORE THE GNATS, A BIRD

i.

Tybalt Ward hadn't always been Tybalt Ward. After the squalling and the cleaning and the being held for the first time, about an hour after he'd been born, his parents had looked at their little boy and named him Tyrone. Had signed the Birth Certificate affixing that name to him.

Seven pounds five ounces, black hair, brown skin. Other baby human features. He wore the name Tyrone and tried to make it him for nearly twenty-five years of his life.

It was a few years after graduating from the Seattle Institute of Business and Economics that he decided he could no longer live as Tyrone. He had changed his name to Tybalt because men named Tyrone don't ever get taken seriously when it comes to obtaining employment in positions of power. And power was what Tybalt had always wanted. Most of all, he had changed his name because he was named after his father, and he had no longer wanted that association.

He had wanted to take the name John, simply because it was the most plain, unassuming name. Johns were everywhere, always in suits and carrying important things and introducing themselves to everyone with 'Hi, I'm John Someoneimportant' after a firm-yet-not-too-overbearing handshake. But he decided not to do that out of regard for his mother, who would always call him Ty, no matter how much he told her that the name was a hinderance and a laughable trope. When he had mentioned to his mother that he was considering changing his name to John, she had screamed, 'TTTTTYYYYYYYYYYYYYYYYYYYYYYYYYY!' so loudly that he thought he would never hear the sound of his name again, no matter what he decided it would be.

Eventually, he chose the name Tybalt because it was ambiguous, and he needed a name that would allow for his mother to still refer to him as Ty.

Tyrell, Tyrod, Tyreek, those names would never allow him to obtain a high-powered job. Would never allow him to advance in life.

Tyrone certainly wouldn't have gotten the job at Helping Hand Home and Auto Insurance. Tyrone had known that jobs like the one he held now – as Tybalt – weren't attainable to guys like him after he had graduated from his Business program with Honors, and had subsequently experienced rejection after rejection from prospective employers based on his resume alone. The resume that had *Tyrone* right there at the very top of it.

Helping Hand would have seen the name Tyrone on a resume and likely thrown it in the garbage like so many had before them.

By the time he had applied for the position of Senior Sales Manager at Helping Hand Home and Auto Insurance, he had been Tybalt for nearly half a decade. The very same resume that had been mainly ignored during his first few years out of school had landed him five interviews and two job offers within months of his name change. That was when he knew for sure. And this knowledge had deadened a part of him. Made him a cynical and bitter man.

He had always understood that life wasn't fair, but he didn't want to accept this piece of confirmation. On some level he had always hoped it was a coincidence that he couldn't get a response to his resume. Bad timing every single time. Something like that. When it was confirmed that this hadn't been the case, he had been devastated by just how unfair it all truly was.

Years later, to Tybalt, this unfairness of the very nature of life wasn't something worth spending too much time being upset about. He had eventually understood, admittedly in a dark sort of way, that the unfairness of life could be counter-balanced. The scales could be tipped back in his direction. And he wasn't simply going to settle for being on equal footing with those who had spent so much time on the other side of the scale. He was going to learn every damn trick in the book until he and his career took off. Then he would make the entire world tilt in his direction.

He had chosen the name Tybalt because he believed that smart white men in positions of power would think he had come from the sort of parents who had shared an appreciation for William Shakespeare, and that would make those powerful white men far more likely to let him through the door. Once in, he would charm his way into staying.

He had chosen the name Tybalt because Tyrone Ward had always thought that Romeo Montague was a weakling and a fool, and had rooted for the Capulets. There were too many women in the world to get so locked onto only one after such a short period of time. Ty Ward believed that love at first sight was simply guilt dressed prettily for those not self actualized enough to understand that it's okay to want to fuck someone you've only just met. Desperately.

Romeo was a fool because he had decided not to survive, all because of some chick he barely knew.

It was mainly the suicide that had caused him to lose all respect for the character of Romeo.

You don't want to get Tybalt Ward started on the subject of suicide.

Bethany Helmsley had gotten him started on that very subject on her last day in the office. That had been a little over two weeks prior to this rare clear and sunny spring day in Daphnis.

On this beautiful day, many of the employees of Helping Hand Home and Auto Insurance were gathered together inside of the building Tybalt was walking toward, about to walk into.

He approached the building on this lovely Saturday afternoon, feeling like everything was bright, and the world was a place where you inhaled and exhaled optimism as well as oxygen.

Most days felt like that to Tybalt. Even the days when the sun was too shy to peek out from behind the seemingly always-prevalent Washington state clouds, the world just seemed so lively and full of promise. He saw adventure everywhere, potential everywhere. He saw the possibility of moving further along in the rat race with every step he took. This was one of the reasons why he hadn't understood Reese Mitchell's decision. Or the decision Bethany had subsequently made a month later after leaving the office that had been a second home to her, perhaps a first home considering she had often sought out the focus and distraction of work to keep the demons of her personal life at bay.

She had taken it – the subject matter of suicide – very seriously, unlike Tybalt. And she had punctuated her point about the seriousness of suicide with the exclamation that had been the taking of her own life.

Bethany's body had been discovered a week prior to this day.

On this day, Mr. Ward stood outside of a cathedral.

The word that was going around among the people who were inside that cathedral – people who were trying very hard to not be overheard gossiping about the dead girl whose last social gathering was being held there – was that Bethany had taken a cocktail of drugs and alcohol. Had died on her couch, mocking sleep.

She hadn't left a note, but her intent had been very obvious. It was a pretty clear-cut case when you looked at it closely. The young woman had a history of struggling with

Chronic Depression and addiction. Her relationship with her brother had been strained due to his own drug use, and her parents had died before she had reached adulthood. If you added the recent losses of her last two closest friends, along with being fired from her job, to the horror story that had already been her life... well, to some, suicide started to seem like an understandable option.

Suicide can sometimes be a catching thing. A deathly contagion. Somewhere along the line the idea of it had jumped from Reese to Bethany, and she had followed the lead of the man who was dearest to her. That was the agreed upon theory, the gathered mourning had decided. That was what made sad and sorrowful sense.

There were other theories being bandied about, regarding not so much the *how* she died but the why. They whispered to each other ideas they had about what might have made her do such a thing. They were sad, yes, extremely, but they were curious. Curiosity takes precedence over all emotions, and sadness only fuels it.

Suicidal motive, it was the thing that everyone just *needed* to know.

Many of those within the cathedral – the ones who *needed* to know – had been accepting as truth the growing speculation that she and Mr. Ward had been involved. They believed it was the way he'd dumped and fired Bethany that had driven her to her end. There were rumors about him having sex with some of his underlings in the past. And he was known for being cold and dismissive. The mourners whispered to themselves that it was Mr. Ward's need for cold, dismissive sex that had probably done her in. An express trip straight over the edge for Bethany Helmsley, courtesy of Mr. Tybalt Ward.

Tybalt wasn't aware of these latter rumors as he stood opposite this gathering of people – many of whom were his underlings. People who were, at that very moment, whispering about him, with only a door and brick and mortar and the

Power of Christ between them. He was focused on his breathing, aware that there could be discomfort ahead, but readying himself to handle it like he handled everything else, like a professional. He saw this as a new beginning. He had needed an out for the Bethany situation. He had gotten too deeply involved with her even after realizing she couldn't be groomed for The Lifestyle.

He had hoped that she would have been accepting of his involvement in The Lifestyle, but after her reaction to seeing him with the maid, Sakura, that Sunday, he had known that could never have been the case.

Bethany had been nice to have around. Fun in a way that he didn't find with the others. She was a salesperson who shared some of his same drive and hunger and desire. Or so he had thought. And then this.

When he had been informed of her passing, he'd been more disappointed than anything else. He had resolved that he would treat it like any other suicide. A choice someone made to take the easy way out. Not something to be mourned.

He stood outside of the cathedral doors, preparing to pretend to mourn. Breathing with purpose.

He thought of Mantra Number 5:

Before you act, inhale and exhale until you're relaxed.

He thought of Mantra Number 6:

Do not allow the things which you cannot control to take control of you.

He felt, truly, as though there was nothing he could do to improve this situation, therefore it would be pointless to beat himself up over it. He didn't think much about what he could have done to have prevented this all from happening to begin with, however. As far as he was concerned, two consenting adults had entered into a consenting adult situation, and one of them had forgotten the risks of being involved sexually with others of the human species.

Hurt is part of the human experience. How one handles that hurt is what defines them. Mantra 18.

Tybalt had tried to explain his perspective to Bethany. He had hoped that by showing the absolute control he had over his maid, by sending her to the closet, that Bethany would see just how different she was from the maid. How she could have ruled as his number one woman, even if he decided to one day obtain a Harem.

She hadn't even tried to hear him out. Hadn't responded to his calls or texts later that Sunday. When he had found out about Reese's death that same evening, he'd understood that things were over for good. He hadn't seen her or heard from her again until the day she had made a spectacle of the both of them at the office. The day she had made it necessary for him to fire her.

Then she had ended her own life, not a survivor but a quitter. That had made it easier for him to get over her. She had been weak, and she would have poisoned him and his brand had she stuck around, not complying, threatening to reveal his secret sexual proclivities to the world. When he thought of it this way, what she had done was a relief in a sense.

Death is the cleanest breakup a person can ever have.

He had paid for all of the details. For a price, he had received the information regarding Bethany's death. Had used his connections with The Fold to find out the names of the paramedics who had been on the scene when she'd been found, and which of those was most likely to give up information that probably shouldn't be giving up to anyone who wasn't next of kin. The paramedic he had made contact with was a man in his mid-forties with an opioid addiction and money management problems.

The two had met in a coffee shop in Puyallup, down the street from a movie theatre that Tybalt had fond memories of. What he had learned from that paramedic – after presenting him with an envelope full of a week of happy nights – was that

Bethany's cat, Yoda, had gotten to her body before her landlord had found her and called for the death cab. The cat hadn't been fed for two days before it decided to make a meal out of the face of its only owner, the woman who had referred to herself as a proud cat mom all over her social media accounts because of Yoda. She had provided for her cat baby even after the very end.

For Bethany, the chances of an open casket funeral had been slim.

What Tybalt had been told by the paramedic after tests had been run, was that Bethany had overdosed on a combination of pain killers, alcohol and Fentanyl, with some marijuana for good measure.

Tybalt may have been the first to whisper this fact publicly, shortly after learning this information.

What he had really wanted to know from the paramedic was whether she had left a note. A note, perhaps, with his name somewhere on it. He was relieved when he learned she hadn't. Note or not, the only three logical results of any autopsy would be accidental overdose, murder or suicide. The latter seeming most likely, the paramedic had let him know.

Tybalt hadn't expected the man to have an answer when he'd asked how they had come to the conclusion of suicide so quickly, and how they had ruled out the other options.

In the proper numerical value, the paramedic had politely asked for at least two more nights of living on a cloud in exchange for this additional information. Tybalt had reached into his pocket and begrudgingly acquiesced, handing over another wad of bills. The paramedic explained that, even though she hadn't left an official suicide note, the rumor was that the last text messages sent from Bethany's phone had been to her dead friend, Reese. The cell phone found near her body had been a loaner device – a temporary replacement for the phone she had smashed while trying to throw it into Tybalt's face. She hadn't bothered to lock the loaner phone, and the medics on the scene were able to see quite a bit before the police had taken the device.

The word was that all of the messages to Reese were apologies, expressions of remorse. Statements indicating that she expected them to reunite at some point. Maybe soon. In addition to that, her blood alcohol level was up to .22%, nearly three times past wasted, and she had enough drugs in her to 'damn near sedate a rhino', as the paramedic had put it. 'Either she was trying to die, or she stopped caring about living. It's all the same,' the paramedic had added before leaving with Tybalt's money and heading directly to purchase many of the same items that had killed the woman he had just been discussing.

Tybalt had paid handsomely for all of these details, and each detail was worth every dollar. Each one made dealing with her death easier.

Now, a few days later, relaxed and ready to act, Tybalt Ward opened the doors to the cathedral that would be the funeral site for one Bethany Lydia Helmsley – born a year, dead a year too close to that she had been born.

ii.

Not all funerals are inherently sad events. This funeral, however, was the very illustration of grief.

Mr. Ward saw a dozen or so people in the narthex of the church, most of whom he recognized from work. His subordinates. He surveyed them swiftly – saw heads bowed, shoulders hunched, faces in hands. These were men and women leaning on each other in a very literal way.

Edith Myers – the woman who many of the young sales brokers jokingly called 'mom' – was actually wailing, the fabric of her blouse twisted and crinkled in her chubby fists. She was leaning against Joseph Barry, salesman of the month this month. Joseph looked upward and away from the wailing woman, both embarrassed and in mourning. No one in the vicinity of Edith made eye-contact with one another. They were all shuffling their feet or searching in their pockets for nothing in particular. Adjusting clothing that was already in pristine order.

Tybalt still didn't quite understand. To him, this was a girl who had been tormented, who had wanted to be released from that torment. He knew that people would be upset, yes, but they raved and wailed as though she were some sort of a victim. He didn't understand that whatsoever.

He hadn't initially intended to attend this funeral. He hadn't attended Reese's burial even though most of the sales team had gone in a show of support of each other, and of Betts. He didn't believe that suicides should be mourned, but he felt compelled to attend Bethany's funeral, perhaps because of the months-long affair he'd had with her. Or, more likely, because the company was taking a major hit on social media, and he believed that it might make Mr. Johjima feel a bit more at ease to know that Tybalt was there to handle things and support the rest of his team. He hadn't heard from the owner and CEO during this entire ordeal, and Tybalt knew not to contact him directly. There had been emails about the situation, however. Instructions for the Daphnis branch of Helping Hand, through Human Resources, from head office and the management types that ranked below Mr. Johjima but above Tybalt Ward.

There had been talk of changes to be made, the sounds of which Tybalt wasn't certain he liked. There had even been talk of implementing a Mental Health First Aid program for all employees at Helping Hand Home and Auto Insurance.

'*Mental Health First Aid?*' he had asked himself aloud in a tone two octaves higher than his norm as he'd read one of the emails from Head Office. His face had screwed up, squeezed by the hands of incredulity. He didn't even know what Mental Health First Aid meant, or would look like, but he wasn't interested. He understood, however, that he would have to pretend to be very interested and engaged in any Mental Health program Mr. Johjima suggested or approved of, lest he risk losing his standing with the owner.

The social media trolls had been out in full force, wondering about the mental health conditions at Triple H & A Insurance. Two suicides in roughly a month within the same office of one of the largest insurance companies in North America; the story had gone from the relatively small city of Daphnis, Washington to the rest of the country in a blink. And while neither of the suicides had implicated the company directly as a cause for their death, their families were curious and upset. Issues at work were assumed. Whispered of. Taken as fact. Which meant damage control for Tybalt, starting with making an appearance at the funeral and looking like he was hurt and full of sorrow about all of this.

And here he was.

Only a few people noticed the new entrant when he had first walked through the doors of the cathedral. But their responses had been so abrupt and violent that others had taken notice of them, and had subsequently taken notice of what they were reacting to. Eventually, all eyes of those in the foyer were focused on Tybalt. On Mr. Ward in his double-breasted charcoal suit, black tie, blacker shirt. The blood-red rose poking out of the suit's front pocket, covering his heart.

Ty surveyed the room, meeting each set of eyes that were locked – laser-like – on him. He nodded at each person, especially Edith, doing his best to look solemn as he did so, fighting the urge to check his gaudy gold watch. He already wanted to leave despite the fact that the funeral hadn't started. Tybalt had made it a habit of always being early, as per Mantra 7:

Early is on time, on time is late, and late is unacceptable.

No one in the foyer returned the solemn nods being doled out by Tybalt. They only continued to stare. They gawked and whispered, this time with more volume.

"I *told* you he would show up."

"He just doesn't have a clue."

Whispered,

"What an asshole."

"Is this guy for real?"

Whispered,

"How could he think this would be a good idea?"

"Ugh. Look at those fucking shoes."

Then came one voice, louder, to Tybalt,

"Mr. Ward, I think it may be best if you just turn around and head on back through those doors."

This was from Heath Carlton, one of Tybalt's best salespeople. He was the largest of them, the most physically imposing. His lifestyle involved sales, cocaine, the gym, and long nights out with other well-toned, party-oriented young men.

Don't even get Tybalt started on *that*. How a man could choose other men instead of women was beyond him. But when it came to those matters, he followed one of his credos. Mantra 30:

Separate business from pleasure. Another's pleasure is not your business.

Not minding one's own business in matters of sex only led to unnecessary conflict, and *unnecessary conflict is counterproductive* (Mantra 27).

Tybalt had no idea how counterproductive things were about to get as Heath took a step out of the gathered mourners toward him. Not in a threatening manner, but rather like a hostage negotiator trying to talk a lunatic out of making a decision he can't come back from.

To Tybalt, it was Heath who was making a decision he would live to regret.

"I'd watch my tone, were I you, Mr. Carlton." He then addressed the entire group assembled in the foyer. The moment he spoke, his words were all there was. His form had magnetized every pupil in the place. All attention was his.

"I'm well aware that things were... tense towards the end with Bethany and I, but she and I worked... closely together on several projects, and I believe I'm due the same chance to pay my respects as the rest of you. She wasn't a spiteful person. She wouldn't have held what happened at the end against me for all of time. I would hope that the rest of you could carry a bit of her lack of ego and her sense of forgiveness with you. I've battled with what happened between the two of us, played it over and over in my head, and asked for forgiveness in my prayers." Tybalt hadn't said a prayer in over a decade. "And I believe that she is here with us in spir–"

He registered the impact before his ears alerted him to the footsteps that had been rapidly approaching.

Impact against the entire right side of his body.

Impact against the ground.

There were gasps, shouts, piercing exclamations.

Tybalt rolled over slowly from his left side and onto his back, some of the air had been forcefully removed from his lungs by the ground he had crashed onto.

"Get. The fuck. Out." This was from a young man he did not recognize, but could still identify based on the familiar pouty mouth and dark features that he shared with Bethany, the dead girl who could only be his older sister.

Tybalt began figuring out how best to deal with this current situation, summoning Mantra 3:

Calculate. Analyze what has happened; formulate what happens next.

He had inched his way up onto his elbows. He registered the fog of silence that had returned, settling uncomfortably upon the foyer of the cathedral while he slowly gathered back his air. Every functioning eye watched him raptly. He was calculating.

He outweighed the young man who had spear-tackled him. He was taller, had a longer reach. Tybalt had studied boxing, kick-boxing and a variety of martial arts upon his graduation from college. Along with meditation, combat sports had always been a helpful form of discipline and release for him. They had helped him overcome a great many frustrations, mainly the residue of his childhood.

He was calculating.

The young man had hit him first, had initiated the violence. Anything that Tybalt did from there on out would be deemed self-defence. And he could do several things from this position on his elbows, below the brother Helmsley who hovered above Tybalt with his finger pointed just a foot away from the fallen man's face.

He could have reached for that finger and snapped it before the boy – or so Tybalt thought of him – realized what was going on. He could have bypassed the finger and grabbed at his wrist, twisting it in a very specific way that would have caused the nerves to make it feel as though the young man's wrist were at the epicenter of an explosion. He could have shattered that wrist altogether. Or simply pulled the boy down and placed the last survivor of Bethany's family in a triangle chokehold.

He could have put the boy into a guillotine.

Calculating.

A leg sweep, then an armbar would have worked just fine. An Oma Plata. Tybalt could have twitched and been on top of the young mourning man, grounding and pounding him into oblivion.

Front headlock into a gator roll. Anaconda Chokehold. There were so many options. The kid would either scream or choke in any situation except for one. The one Tybalt chose.

He crawled backward, toward the exit. He got up slowly, adjusting his suit, looking with barely constrained annoyance at the two bare spots where the buttons of his jacket had once been. The red rose that had covered his heart was in pulpy smears on the floor.

Dead silence, until he spoke.

"I guess I was mistaken," Tybalt Ward said to the mourners in the narthex. The commotion had brought many others out from the nave of the church. Whispers and inquisitive murmurs had begun to override the previous silence. "My apologies. I didn't mean to cause a scene. My condolences to you all."

The young man who had tackled him made a move as though he were going to attack him once more, but was restrained by Heath and several of the other mourners.

The whispers and murmurs had now turned into full on chat and chatter. He ignored them all.

Tybalt turned, head held high, and exited the church.

iii.

One of the calculations that had gone through Tybalt's mind was the mental state of the young man who had attacked him.

He was now fifteen minutes removed from the cathedral and was walking down the streets of uptown Daphnis, a part of the city he hadn't walked through in years. For once, he felt aimless, a bit uncertain. He was invoking Mantra 4:

Recalculate. Check your work. Being correct in the present only helps with being correct in the future.

He went over what had happened again, and again was convinced he had made the correct choice. It's not that he was intimidated by the boy, with his pointing finger and crazed eyes and eagerness to lash out. Quite the contrary, the wilder the opponent, the easier to tame him. What Ty had considered when thinking of how to react was the fact that this young man was a bomb that would eventually go off, destroying himself without Tybalt having to lift a finger. It would have done Mr. Ward's image no good if he was known as the guy who kicked the shit out of the last remaining member of a mostly dead family, the sister recently murdered by her own hand. He had remembered the little details that Betts had told him about her family between all of the moaning and groaning that was the majority of their verbal interaction after that initial night of so much talking. One of those details was that she had a younger brother, and the two of them had been just the two of them since their parents had died while on a vacation in Mexico when Bethany had been in her late teens. She and her brother had fended for each other as best they could, eventually losing their parents' home and having no choice but to live in parts of the city that two teenagers should have avoided entirely.

They had both developed drug and alcohol problems along the way. Bethany had eventually been able to quit, which should have been a good thing. However, it was her quitting that had damaged their relationship, because her brother could not. The two had grown apart over the last few years due to her brother's increasing drug use and reckless behavior.

Tybalt had seen the remorse in the young man's eyes, the hurt, the wanting to expel those deeply dark feelings, but not knowing how. In regards to the overdose of his sister, the guy was probably dealing with as much guilt as the person who had supplied her with the drugs she had overdosed on might have been. An ass-kicking would only propel the boy even faster toward his own inevitable suicide. More importantly, to Tybalt, kicking that young man's ass would have been career suicide. And there would be no one to mourn that but himself.

So, he had left, and hoped that his being attacked and walking away would make him a more sympathetic figure in this entire ordeal. He knew he could come off as brusque to his employees at times, which was why he had wanted this show of his maturity – of his ability to turn the other cheek – to change their opinions, even if only slightly.

He continued walking for a time, reacquainting himself with each street he was on the way one does when on any always-thriving street in a core area of a city one hasn't visited in years. His surroundings looked different but similar to what he remembered from the days after college when he had been far more likely to take long walks down busy streets.

He had grown, the city had grown, but so much of it was still familiar. There was new paint on old buildings. Different signage on the same recycled businesses. So much had changed. So much was as it always had been.

Tybalt found himself stopped in front of a bar that he could have sworn he'd been to before, back when this entire strip had been a major part of his life after he'd moved to Daphnis from Seattle upon his graduation. Back when he was still partying, still being rejected by employers, still trying to figure out what to do next.

Back when he was a young man named Tyrone. Before Tybalt had murdered Tyrone and steered straight onto a course that would lead to power and wealth and all the potential connections that money could buy. And even some that money couldn't.

When he thought of his former life, of Tyrone, he usually focused on the present moment and pushed that thought aside. Allowing it briefly, but letting it know it wasn't welcome back in his mind. Tyrone was a man gone and buried. Though for some reason, perhaps it was all of the actual death lately, Tybalt was feeling nostalgic. A drink in this bar, for Tyrone, couldn't hurt. He thought of Mantra 22, his least favorite and least used:

Without roots there can be no growth.

It called for one to delve deeply into their past, to be in touch with not only their younger selves, their former selves, but their parents, their grandparents, their ancestors. Tybalt thought of Tyrone's parents and scowled. He thought of his grandfather, and that did nothing to change his countenance.

Tybalt had spent most of his life trying to hack away his roots, considering himself the apple which had fallen far from the tree and had kept on rolling.

Even now, as he stood on the street staring at a familiar and unfamiliar bar, Tybalt felt a great deal of shame in thinking about the men who had contributed to his genes.

On that bus ride that had changed so much for so many people, he had talked about his family to Bethany. He had described his grandfather as a caring, doting hippie who had bravely faced cancer on his own in order to save his family from prolonged grief. What Tybalt hadn't mentioned was that his grandfather had been a chain-smoker and a high functioning alcoholic. He had hid his bad habits from his daughter well enough, but would turn into a drunken chimney the moment she was gone and he was left in charge of her boy.

He hadn't been a kindly old man dying way before his time, eager to impart his mortal wisdom on his grandson. He was a crotchety old drunk whose idea of quality time with his pre-teen grandson was day-drinking while chain-smoking blunts and cigarettes, and shooting guns in the forest with the boy somewhere nearby. He hadn't been a bad man, and Tybalt had even enjoyed some of their time together, but at the end of the day the man had smoked himself into an early grave. Had had no self control, even in the face of death. That showed a lack of character. To Tybalt, that was a sign of weakness. There could be no room for that sort of weakness in his life.

His mother's father had been fundamentally flawed. His own father had been no better.

His father had also been weak. Tybalt had understood this only years after he had first been told the man had been killed in battle. This had been after he'd found out about the war his dad had actually died in.

He had told Bethany that his father had died at war because he had been told the same when he was a child. For years he had truly believed that his father was a decorated soldier. Then he became a teenager who had recently watched his grandfather discreetly drink and smoke himself to death. That version of Tyrone had become more cynical, more questioning. Suspicious. He had developed whatever part of the thought process that allows for genuine critical thinking and had applied this critical thinking to the story of his father's death. Eventually, he asked his mother questions like 'Where are his medals?', 'Where is his uniform?', 'Can I meet his former officers?', and received answers that all boiled down to 'It was a hard time for all of us and I'd like to put it behind us, Ty. Let your father rest peacefully.'

Ty had accepted this at first, taken his mother's word that his father had been a heroic soul who had died trying to protect his country. She wanted to leave it in the past, and, out of respect for her, he had left it there.

Then, over a decade later, came the age of Google. The internet and its search engines that made the past an ever-present thing. One day, well after he had gone off to business school, Tybalt found himself in his dorm room preparing for his impending graduation by applying for jobs, not wanting to work on his final assignment which was due in two days. He had decided to Google himself out of equal parts boredom and need for distraction. He had typed in 'Tyrone Ward.' Several photos of several different black men had popped up. He perused through them, wondering just how many unspectacular men with his unspectacular name were out there, making him even less spectacular with their very existence.

Then a familiar photo had popped up.

Tyrone Ward.

Senior.

His father.

He had clicked on the image. It wasn't any picture he had remembered ever seeing, though he hadn't seen many photos of his father. The memory of his dad, until that point, mostly existed within a framed photo the family had kept on their mantle or a side table, depending on which low-rent shithole they occupied at the time. It was a photo that Tybalt had always believed he would keep with him when his mother no longer had any use for it. It was one of the few items of his father's he believed he could inherit – just a still image of the man he was.

A picture says a thousand words, unless it is used as a blank slate. A blank slate is what that photo of Tyrone's father had been. His mother had filled it with stories about military bravery, about a hero of a human being dying to defend the freedoms of his fellow man. A very young Ty had filled in the gaps of those stories, making his father the bravest and best dad who had died way too early that there ever was.

He had hung onto those stories until the day he had Googled himself and found an image of his father, one that led to a website featuring a news report that said:

Drug Dealer Gunned Down in Long Standing Seattle Turf War.

Ty's father had died fighting for a corner, not for his country. A pointless death. A pointless man.

And Ty had been named after him.

After that point, whenever he thought of that framed photo of his father, he filled in the formerly blank slate with a thousand words he found to be fitting. Words like: stereotype, liar, thug, shame, disgrace, villain. Words of that variety.

Everything that his mother (and that picture of his father) had raised him to be was a lie.

He had started meditating shortly after all of that. It was his way to deal with the anger caused by the memories of his grandfather and the truth about his dad.

But that's not the sort of story you tell a girl on a bus who you're trying to sleep with.

The meditation had saved his life by keeping him calm. Preventing him from becoming like the out of control men his father and grandfather had been. He had studied the art of meditation alongside his studies of the martial arts. Tybalt had become a student of numerous elements of many Asian cultures. He had a fascination with what he thought was the main tenet within these cultures: the discipline, the self-control.

Before he had decided to become his own father to this newer version of himself, the lie inside the picture of his actual father had been the best role model he'd ever had. Once that version of his father had been destroyed by the truth, Tybalt had allowed himself to move on, no longer interested in his family tree or its roots.

He had long ago considered himself the singular root that would inspire whatever growth was necessary for his success. Yet, here he was, thinking of that young man who had once been him, now dead. Ty wondered if that meant he had committed suicide, in a sense, as well.

Every once in a while he felt he needed to do things for the person he used to be, if for no other reason than to remind himself of how far he'd come. And of what to never go back to.

Now he stood in front of this familiar structure with unfamiliar signage, indulging memories that belonged to the dead stranger he had once been.

This bar was one of the many establishments built side by side by side in that fire hazard kind of way that old strips of homes and businesses had often been constructed. It was a little hole in the wall he was certain he'd been surrounded by on many of those nights when he wasn't quite sure who he was or who he could become.

Ty looked down at his weary feet. They had walked him here all on their own it seemed, and now he knew why. His feet were weary because of his choice of footwear – red crushed velvet loafers. He had loved them when he'd put them on a few hours ago for the funeral. Now he felt a bit ridiculous for having worn them. He had thought the shoes would add a bit of flair to the drab nature of the rest of his outfit. Had thought they would be a subtle bit of brightness during a gloomy occasion. Now he wondered why he'd thought such foolish things. Why had he thought it would be a good idea for him to show up at the funeral to begin with?

For one of the few times in recent years, Tybalt felt more like Tyrone. He felt a creeping, uneasy doubt climb its way into his brain and rest there, gnawing. Doubt, presenting itself as a new and unbidden nuisance. Doubt, pestering, fluttering in his mind.

Like a gnat.

It was then that he remembered Reese Mitchell's words, spoken from Bethany Helmsley's raging mouth. Both of them now dead. He remembered her shouting at him, staring with her big, brown watery eyes at her telephone, at the words that Reese had decided upon to be among his last:

It's like a gnat's inside your head... an evil gnat that wants you dead.

He shook away the words, hoped to shake away this new feeling of surrealness, of being out of control.

For the first time in a long time his life had fallen from the path he had carefully laid out, brick by brick. He was now walking down a different road, familiar yet foreign. And his feet hurt.

It was his feet that told him to stop. To take a break, to go into this dive bar and take a load off. Have a drink, think, recalculate, recalibrate. He had been through worse, he reminded himself.

He looked at the neighborhood around him. The day sparkled, the sidewalks teemed with people enjoying the sort of weather they didn't get often enough. Yet he felt gray and alone standing there in front of this dive. There were other places to drink, restaurants where his suit – missing buttons or not – would not feel so out of place. But it was this bar that had told his feet to stop. To come in and allow his new self to be his old self and try this new place that had once been a part of his old history. Before it had been remodelled and renamed, just like him.

He couldn't remember what the bar had been called previously, but he was certain it hadn't been what was spelled out on the signage now:

The Black Bird Bar and Grill.

Taking a deep breath, he removed his jacket, for once not caring that the back and underarms of his shirt were ringed with sweat.

Releasing that breath, and relieving himself of his pretentions, Tybalt Ward walked down a short flight of steps and into the Black Bird Bar and Grill.

iv.

It was a hole in the wall. A dive bar. You've seen it. Take a walk in every downtown, or uptown, or midtown in every city in the United States of America. Stand in any part of town in any town in all the Westernized World. Pick a direction. Spit. You'll hit one of these places.

Bars (some including Grills), Taverns, Pubs, Alehouses.

These are the sorts of places that specialize in a certain thing or two – a certain thing or two that draws in just enough regulars who really appreciate that certain thing or two enough to keep these types of places open – and not much else. Sometimes, that certain thing is to supply you with a drink you can afford. Something cheap, something stiff.

That's what had brought the young Tyrone Ward here all those years ago. It was what Tybalt he was looking for now.

He felt a lot larger all of a sudden, walking down the four-step flight of stairs that led into the slightly subterranean bar (and grill). Or was it that he remembered this place as being larger back when he had been a much smaller, less significant character.

He surveyed the small, dim bar, always keeping a vigilant eye out for unsavory types. He saw none because he saw no one. For a moment, Tybalt believed the establishment to be empty. The hostess' podium was host-less, the bar just behind it to his left was neither tended nor kept. In what could be considered a dining area, several rows of tables lined the wall to Tybalt's right. The first few were empty, and Tybalt began to wonder if the place was actually open. It was still pretty early in the da–

His eyes passed over a spot of white so bright it was nearly a scream in the semi-dark of the establishment. The restaurant was open. Tybalt wasn't alone in there.

His eyes rested on a man sitting in front of a woman at a table in the far corner of this little strip of an establishment. Tybalt wondered how it was possible he hadn't spotted this man as soon as he'd walked in. The man wore a trench coat of an unrealistically white hue. Tybalt, usually not much for metaphor or fanciful imagery, suddenly got the picture, in his head, of thread woven out of the bright white clouds that only exist on days containing the bluest of skies.

This man was wrapped in nimbus, draped in atmosphere. His skin was the same coconut complexion as Tybalt's, making the stark white of his coat even more apparent. It seemed to illuminate the gloom of the restaurant that surrounded him, casting light on the companion who sat in front of him.

Light she almost seemed to absorb.

From his perspective at the entrance of the establishment, all Tybalt could see was the back of her head. Her hair.

Black as absence.

Black as void.

So dark it seemed to be the epicenter of the dimness that filled this bar.

The man wearing the bright white coat appeared to be agitated. His posture rigid. His face a scowl when his lips weren't moving rapidly. Which they seemed to be, frequently. He was controlling the bulk of whatever conversation the two were having.

Short pause. Scowl. Rapid lip movement. Repeat.

There seemed to be a glint of something shiny from behind his lips that became more noticeable the more animated he appeared. He appeared to be exclaiming something that Tybalt couldn't hear over the music in the dimly lit bar. Rock music. Music Tybalt hadn't even noticed until he had tried to overhear the conversation of the animated couple in the corner. It took a moment for him to recognize

Blue Oyster Cult's *Don't Fear The Reaper* before the music transitioned to The Rolling Stones' *Sympathy for The Devil.* He thought this was an odd choice of music, but then again, to him, this was an odd place entirely. Or maybe he was now the odd one. He didn't feel that he belonged, Tyrone, Tybalt, neither of them. Being inside this place hadn't rejuvenated his spirits, hadn't brought him down a positive stretch of memory lane, as he had hoped.

It was the same building, different place.

He was the same body. Different man.

Perhaps it was walking in on what he assumed had to be some sort of marital spat that caused his feelings of unease to rise. That made him feel less than comfortable standing there.

Tybalt was about to turn to go when, as if sensing that he had just been under observation, The Black Man In The White Trench Coat turned and caught Tybalt's eye. Caught it even as Ty was in the process of turning. And Tybalt could not help but re-turn himself toward the table where the couple were having their row, allowing his vision to be reeled into the complete and utter focus of this man clad in a white as bright as madness. His eyes the deep blue of the Atlantic Ocean.

The music slowed in tempo, then in volume, then became inaudible.

Tybalt thought he heard the man's companion say,

"You can't use that tongue on me." Then nothing. No retort. Tybalt wasn't sure why he was so transfixed by this pair, but he was. He was actively eavesdropping, wondering what the man would say in response.

Still nothing.

The two had stopped talking. The woman seemed to stare at her companion while he stared at Tybalt with eyes that shone, even from across the room. It was as though Tybalt's appearance had completely taken away the man's interest in his conversation with his companion.

No one moved and nothing moved and everything stilled.

An eternity passed in the tick of the long hand of the clock.

Tybalt suddenly didn't just feel uneasy, he felt a sense of wrong so intense and deep in his stomach it was as though a malignancy had sprouted in his bowels, germinated, and would be in full deathly bloom if he didn't turn and get out of this dive bar that was so like and so unlike so many places in the Western World.

But as he turned to go, the man staring at him rose. Rose with a haste that bordered on violence, but with a grace that caused him to make no sound. No chair toppled over. No tableware rattled. His black-haired companion didn't so much as flinch.

He stepped into the aisle from behind his table, stepped into the walkway that led straight toward the exit. The exit that Tybalt stood in front of.

The Man was still staring at Tybalt as he marched toward the exit that Tybalt couldn't quite figure out how to run to, or run out of the way of.

He was entranced.

This man, who was taking long and purposeful strides toward Tybalt while staring into his soul, was walking artwork. A sight to behold.

He wore gray denim jeans above black boots waxed to a sheen. He wore a white button-down shirt above and tucked into his jeans. Between his jeans and shirt, was a large, heavily adorned belt buckle. It was a silver number 8 with four blue star-shaped diamonds within it (two in the top loop, two in the bottom loop).

Atop and around it all, he wore his Coat of Clouds.

He was somehow, suddenly, only feet away from Tybalt. And Tybalt, who should have been calculating, was wondering why that malignant feeling in his stomach had now turned into unbidden arousal for the man who strode toward him.

This was a feeling Ty had never experienced before.

This was a feeling counter to all of his personal philosophies and beliefs. He fought it off.

He tried to regain his composure.

He calcula—

But it was too late for plans and calculations, The Trench-Coated Man was upon him, still staring into his eyes with those unusually blue gemstones.

Tybalt was unnerved. His feet felt as if they had walked away, abandoning his body, leaving him behind on legs that didn't quite know how to balance without them.

Tybalt dropped his jacket, he felt he would need both hands. He went to raise his fists to fend off blows. He managed to move the stumps that had once been connected to his traitorous feet into a position that would allow for him to counter a strike.

And then The Black Man In The White Trench Coat walked past him. Though not before giving his head a disappointed shake in the direction of Tybalt. It was only then, at their point of passing, that he broke eye-contact. Ty felt as though a line, a rope, some means of connection, had been severed.

The Black Man In The White Trench Coat opened the door. Tybalt turned in time to see the wind cause The Man's trench coat to billow and pulse as it flowed behind him.

The light from the door swallowed him, and, once the strange man's silhouette cleared, Tybalt had to raise both hands to fend off the sun before the door swung back. Closed.

And Tybalt's eyes began the process of readjusting to the dimness of his surroundings.

V.

A now-shaken Tybalt looked back from the door to the table The Trench-Coated Man had walked from. It seemed as though his companion had yet to move. Her focus continued to be fixated directly ahead of her, as if the man who had been there hadn't parted from her company. Tybalt could still only see her hair, the color of oblivion.

It was odd, all of this. The untended bar, the mostly empty establishment. The entire scene was off and off-putting. And that was enough for him to want to leave.

His feet had cowered back to his legs, and he was able to maneuver his body enough to bend down and pick up the jacket he had dropped when he thought he would have to defend himself for the second time in an afternoon that was now feeling like one long week.

He stood up warily, almost woozily, the intense stare of that... unusual man seemed to have left him slightly discombobulated. Now he needed air, needed to leave. He stood erect, looked down at his jacket as he dusted it off, irritated that such an expensive part of his wardrobe had touched this disgusting bar's floor. He went to take one more look at the back of The Trench-Coated Man's companion and nearly fell as he saw that she was immediately in front of him. Right there. The two were nearly face-to-face. He hadn't heard her footsteps. Hadn't thought it would be possible for her to cross that distance in the time during which he had taken his eyes off of her. He thought it might have been someone else, but it was the hair that made him certain that this could undoubtedly be no one other than that man's companion. Hair the color of absence and void and oblivion shrouding a face that, to Tybalt, was all at once and more suddenly than her appearance in front of him, absolutely everything.

This time it was his knees that threatened to desert him as he stared into eyes the color of both blue ice and, at once, blue fire.

She extended her hand to shake his. He took it thankfully, steadied himself. Shook it. Her hand was hot. Electric. That pulsing heat seemed to pour out of her and enter into him. He felt his pulse accelerate, his blood beginning to flow faster. He flushed deeper than ever, even as he tried not to, and hoped that she wouldn't notice in the dim lighting. Though even before that thought had run its complete path across his mind, he realized that he could easily tell how flushed she was. Or perhaps she was just deeply tanned. Sunburned rouge. Either way, he found the reddish hue of her skin to be an attractive feature.

He struggled not to look at the rest of her attractive features, which meant he had to look overtop her head, because, below that vantage, her attractive features were everywhere.

He had glimpsed full lips painted black, with perfection painted all over the face around those lips. Her clothing seemed to be made out of fresh coats of paint as well.

The woman wore black jeans with red cross-stitching at the hips. Her midriff, tanned red, was exposed nearly entirely. And above that stretch of flawless flesh was a too-small black T-Shirt, upon which was the word *Novoselic*. He had trouble making out the word because the swell of her breasts had badly distorted it.

Tybalt kicked himself for not having untucked his shirt after removing his jacket. He was close to the point of embarrassment.

He continued to look at the top of her head, thought unsexy thoughts, and prayed she wouldn't notice the developments happening below his belt.

She spoke. Her voice was cooling lava.

"I just wanted to apologize for my brother's behavior."

"Your broth...?" He looked back at the door as if expecting the man who had exited it to be standing there specifically for Tybalt's slack jawed comparison. "I thought he was... never mind. It's just that you two look so different." He would have guessed that she was Spanish, maybe Native American. Or some genealogical mix that would better explain those eyes. That skin. The man who had left the bar was far more likely to be Ty's brother than hers.

They were still shaking hands. A handshake he didn't want to end. When she removed her hand from his, he suddenly felt depleted. It was like some vital part of himself had been in need of her touch to make him feel whole. He needed that touch again. Ty had never felt so unsteady in all of his life.

She put the tip of the index finger of the hand she had removed from his into her mouth, and smiled around it.

"We have different fathers." she responded.

He didn't know what to say.

There was an awkward pause.

He observed her during that uncomfortable silence, saw the blue eyes that were glaciers in her head, remembered the Trench Coated Man's own azure irises, and thought that their mother had to have had the second most beautiful eyes to ever have existed. Second only to her daughter – this woman in front of him who he had no idea just how to speak to.

His lips moved but words did not come out. Gesticulations were gesticulated for no reason other than discomfort.

It was a very long awkward pause.

"Let me buy you a drink," she said, saving him from further looking like an imbecile.

"Oh?" was all he could think to say. She couldn't save him from sounding like an imbecile, unfortunately.

He didn't understand what was happening to him, why he was acting like a ditz. A dullard. He began, slowly, to remind himself of who he was. Tybalt Ward, who had worked his way out of meager beginnings and was well on his way to becoming a self-made millionaire. He reminded himself that he was in command. Always.

He controlled his breathing, slowed his pulse.

He calculated.

Or at least he tried to, but his calculator had malfunctioned and what he wound up saying was,

"I mean, oh...kay." Then he visibly cringed. But she only smiled at him, showing two rows of ten-thousand perfect teeth. She turned to the bartender, whose existence Tybalt had only registered at the same moment she had turned to him, and she put up two fingers like the peace sign, then she pointed those two fingers toward the table that she and her companion had occupied. Tybalt was still struggling to believe the two were related. He briefly wondered if she expected the man to return and was just using Tybalt as a way to further increase his ire. Maybe he was a jealous lover, maybe they had just broken up, maybe he had gone to his car or his home or a Walmart to get some weaponry and was about to come back and mass shoot the entire bar. The guy already had the trench coat for it.

He tried to calculate, but the word 'maybe' always had a way of stalling Tybalt's computations. He prided himself on being a man of certainty. However, in this instance, he wasn't certain of anything, and didn't know what to do whatsoever. Which was why he allowed himself, for one of the few times in his adult life, to be led.

She walked toward the table and he followed without even thinking to do so. His feet were doing their own thing again, this time taking the unthinking Tybalt with them.

The two sat down across from one another. Tybalt was starting to feel more like himself, though nowhere near as confident as he typically would be in a scenario where he had been invited to a table for drinks with a beautiful woman. The invitation alone meant he was at least halfway there. But her beauty created a sort of disarray inside his head. Dizzying would be a word to describe her looks. Disorienting would be another.

She looked at him from beneath her obsidian bangs as he struggled to hold her stare. Her eyes were so beautiful they were nearly painful. The two were silent again, but this time it wasn't so awkward. This time they were drinking each other in while waiting for their beverages.

"What happened?" Now it was his tongue moving without his knowledge or permission. Why would he ask that? Why would he go straight to such a personal question? That was a rookie move, and Tybalt Ward fancied himself a cagey veteran. He braced himself for her to tell him to mind his own business, but she only smiled. His penis shifted in his pants in response.

"We sometimes have disputes over property that each of us believes we are the owner of. We have a... complicated relationship."

"Oh, I'm sorry. I didn't mean to pry." Tybalt was talking around the foot that had found its way into his mouth. He dislodged it and finally focused on not sounding like a lovestruck fool.

Love.

He hadn't ever believed in love outside of the familial type. He had thought it a social construct, an instinct of self-preservation, insurance against winding up with the all-too-dreaded fate of being alone and lonely. He believed that everything people did was done with self-preservation as the underlying motivator. If it didn't in some way benefit the self, then a human wouldn't do it. Love, to Tybalt, was just an embodiment of an individual's selfish desires projected onto someone else who could fulfil those desires.

This had always been his philosophy. His religion.

The Church of Self-Fulfillment.

Take unto thee my burdens as your own. Take unto thee my burdens with your own. But for her, he would take all of the burdens. Hers and his and all the world's. And he would be okay if that meant being crushed by the weight of those burdens in the process.

The feeling he was feeling at this moment was a lifetime of beliefs being shattered. His religion turned to mythology, The Church of Self-Fulfillment debunked. For her, he cared. He loved, he yearned.

"You're not prying, silly. If someone charged at me the way he charged at you, I would want to know what caused it too. No one should have to go through something like that."

The waitress, another person who seemed to pop into existence only when she was acknowledged by the jet-haired girl, appeared with two drinks. He watched as the woman who now owned his senses indicated to the waitress to bring two more.

Then the waitress stopped existing as she walked away.

The woman in front of him was a vacuum, sucking up all of his attention. Nothing mattered outside of her pull. To him, the place was empty. He knew that there were people there, at least a waitress and a bartender, but he could not register them because his mind was fixated on one thing. And everything other than her face – that one thing – was a blur.

He forced his eyes away from the vortex of her face and looked down at the two highball tumblers on the table. Then there were four – the waitress had come back with more drinks. She was instructed to get four more. Immediately. Ty looked down at the table which was slowly filling up with tumblers containing gold liquid, each with a shot-glass of something brown in the middle.

"A Short Trip to Hell." she said. Then she downed glass number one. Chased it with glass number two. "Drink." she insisted, and watched him. Her ice-blue-blue-fire eyes turning him cold and hot in alternating waves. He had never been fond of mixed drinks, and he had a terrible suspicion that the shot glass full of brown in the middle was Jägermeister, which he hated. He drank nonetheless, because that's what she wanted, and he wanted to make her happy.

He felt he might do just about anything to make her happy.

The waitress was wearing out the floor with her back and forth and back and forth from the bar to the table, bringing drinks and taking empties. He had lost count of both of their drink tallies, but knew his companion had to have been ahead of him by a factor of two, maybe even three times more. Then, while she was working on what he estimated was her twentieth drink, she missed her lips and spilled her Short Trip to Hell down her chin and over the front of her shirt. Some of the liquid made its way to her exposed midsection, causing her tanned skin to gleam under the bar's faint light. He would have thought she were drunk if not for the calm smile that spread across her face.

"Whoops," she said, not bothering to take a napkin and dab herself dry. Instead, she licked at the liquid on her chin – her entire chin – with a tongue that Tybalt thought seemed unusual and amazingly long. He nearly melted in his chair. She looked down at her wet shirt. Asked,

"Can you help me with this? In the back room maybe?" She then stood up, turned and walked, seeming to know that his feet would do the thing she wanted them to do. They did. He walked and watched behind her, his pupils a pair of pendulums swaying in time with the movement of her hips. The only thing that drew their attention from her hips was the fact that she was removing her shirt even as the bartender and waitress that may as well have been invisible to Tybalt looked on, watching him walk behind her, saying nothing.

She was a few yards ahead of him, her shirt left behind on the floor. As he stepped over it, he fought the urge to stoop down, pick it up and give it perhaps a hundred thousand good, deep sniffs.

Inhale. Exhale.

He easily defeated that urge when he saw her turn the corner of the bar, reaching with her hands behind her and stretching in that sexy way exclusive to the female form to undo the clasp of her bra. The bra was on the ground by the time she walked through the swinging door that said *Employees Only*.

This time Tybalt insisted that his feet pick up the pace. And with his pants considerably less comfortable than they had been before she had begun her striptease, he jogged into the room after her.

vi.

There were employees there. Only employees, as the door had indicated. And they seemed unnerved by the presence of the bodacious black-haired beauty with the still-moist chin and no clothing over her torso. Her jeans seemed to strain to contain her lower half. The employees looked, unmoving. Stared but didn't stir, as though they were afraid that if they reacted they would be penalized. As though they were expected to pretend that this was business as usual. Or an interlude to the usual business they were accustomed to seeing.

He recalled her mentioning that she and her brother had been in a dispute over property, and wondered if The Black Bird Bar and Grill was a property she owned. It would explain the abundance of unpaid for drinks, and the silent, eerie regard of the staff.

At that point he had followed her through the kitchen, through the staff lounge. Not a single person whom they had passed had said a word. Not a single one of them had blinked.

The two approached their final destination – a chipped and peeling wooden door at the back of the staff lounge. It was old and worn down except for the handle, which was the same black as the woman's hair.

It was the most ornate door handle Tybalt had ever seen, one shaped like the number 8 tipped sideways. Six red gems bejeweled it. And it gleamed like polished jet stone against the faded wood it was embedded into.

He was hesitant to touch it, but when he looked back to tell her this, she only smiled and nodded. He did what those gestures suggested immediately.

With his hand on the doorknob, he felt an energy that both seemed to give and take from him. He held his breath as he opened the door, closed his eyes as he entered the room. He wasn't certain what he had been expecting to see before he opened his eyes, but he was underwhelmed by what was in front of him.

He was looking at a small room that was half-office and half-bedroom. There was a modest corner desk, a twin bed, and little else. Posters and charts and spreadsheets that Tybalt didn't bother to look at were taped onto pock-marked cement walls that were a peeling shade of pale blue and screamed for a new paint job. But all Tybalt was focused on was the woman with the raven black hair whose name he had no clue of. She had walked into the room, stood by the bed, and was peeling the painted layer that was her pants off of her. He found that he was doing the same to his own.

Once she was without any clothing, she bent over on the bed. Tybalt began to salivate, then actually drooled at the sight of all of her. Appetizer, main course, all of her, dessert. She looked at him with her face on the bed and her bottom up in the air behind her. She looked at him from between her naked arm and her naked thigh and her every aperture showing. She said,

"See the world for what it is."

He paused only for a moment before doing as she bade. At least he thought he was doing as she bade. While he hadn't understood what she had said, he was adept at body language, and her body was saying there was no more need for talking, for interpretation.

Here they were.

She had invited him into her world. And he knew that she would be an experience he couldn't imagine. Something that would change his life.

There was a condom in his pants, but his pants were on the floor, right there and also several miles away. He couldn't be bothered with reaching over and getting that piece of protection. Besides, he trusted her. He loved her.

He entered her.

And, somehow, she filled him.

It was ecstasy unlike anything he had felt before. He was at the core of the meaning of the word bliss. It was the most excruciatingly pleasurable feeling in the world. And out of the world. Because when he was in her, deep inside of her, he saw things that couldn't be of this Earth. He closed his eyes and saw a highway, a long road, built upon 4 pillars that stretched out of blue desolation and rose and rose and held this road that looped and turned in the shape of infinity. He saw beings traveling this road. Some were human, some were things that – if he tried to affix descriptive words to – caused his head to hurt profusely.

He saw a door at the edge of the road. The road itself was built along all of the stars of the universe, weaving and looping into an immeasurable number of worlds. And there were things he saw beneath the road, things of a nature so grotesque that, for a moment, even in the middle of the bliss that was the beautiful stranger's body, Tybalt believed he would be better off blind than seeing them for much longer. He would be fine never seeing anything again, he thought, turning his attention back to her, if it meant that for the rest of his life he could simply focus on this bliss.

Which is what he did. He ignored the cascade of confusing images swirling in his mind. He focused on the drug she was, and dosed and dosed and dosed.

He released eventually. Released his seed, released his strength, released his consciousness. The last thing he heard, while passing out even as some of his ejaculate was still vacating him and entering her, was the exclamation she made. He thought for a moment it was a caw, the sound of her pleasure mistaken for a bird.

He smiled as his consciousness flew after that bird into darkness.

vii.

"...a gnat's inside your head. An evil gnat that wants you dead."

Tybalt stirred. Those were the words that had stirred him.

"It's like a gnat's inside your head. An evil gnat that wants you dead."

She was whispering this to him in a sing-song voice, almost chanting, almost incanting.

"It's like a gnat's inside your he—"

"Stop. Why are you saying that?" He had heard words of this nature before, but could no longer place where he had heard them. He'd dismissed them the first time, that much he knew, but this time... This time...

"It was something you were saying, actually. In your sleep."

He blinked until he was able to regain focus. He turned and looked at the person who had just been whispering in his ear. He blinked again, waiting for his eyes to adjust to the lightless room.

It was her, in the bed beside him. It was her, but different. There was something not the same about her eyes. They were still a burning and chilling blue, but there was something shifting in the quality of them. Something unsettling. Something unsettled.

"Now why would you be whispering that in your sleep, Tyrone?"

"I..." He began to respond, until the realization of what she had called him caused his sentence to halt, her words turning to cold, hard fingers that wrapped themselves around his throat and ended his ability to communicate. Other cold, hard fingers traced themselves along his skull and down his spine.

"Why would you be dreaming of such troubling things, Tyrone?"

Again, she said it. Again, the feeling of frosty unease all over his person.

He wracked his brain to remember what her name was. He had a knack for remembering names. A quality that he had worked on purposefully. People always felt a sense of warmth and belonging when you addressed them by their names in situations where it would have been understandable for those names to have been forgotten. Tybalt had used this to his advantage, always reminding people of how they had met, calling them by name and refreshing their memories concerning one chance encounter or another some time ago that had caused him to remember their names forever. At times he would even inject and insert aspects of memories that weren't exactly true. And he would watch them 'remember' these moments fondly. People were so open to suggestion if you made them feel important.

This knack for names was how he knew he hadn't been given hers, and he was certain he hadn't relinquished his. Never would he have introduced himself as Tyrone. No matter how many Short Trips to Hell the two had downed during their brief drink date.

How does she know me? Do I know her? Is all of this some sort of a setup?

He pushed away these uncertain thoughts as he looked over at the woman who had eyes so bright that they turned the room from death-dark to dim. He looked into that brightness and thought how much a fool he had been to have wanted blindness not too long ago. How could he live without ever being able to look into those eyes? He would view all of the horrors of the universe if it meant there was a chance to see her.

Those eyes.

But there was something wrong in them.

Something shifting.

He flashed back to when he had, Once Upon A Time, been in control. He thought now of how far from those days he was. For the first time in over a decade he understood and accepted that control was a thing not reachable. Not to him. Not now. Maybe never again. He was okay with that so long as it was to her that he relinquished it. Control. He was okay with her telling him what to do and when to do it, and he would do it happily with a smile on his face and no questions on his tongue. But she wasn't telling him anything now. Not what to do. Not how she knew his name. Not what her own name was.

"Raveena." The word blew from her mouth like a puff of cigarette smoke. So intoxicating, addictive. Carcinogenic.

"Pardon?" he coughed out, not quite sure what was going on, the sense of Dis-Reality swelling in his head.

"My name is Raveena, though my friends call me Raven. Would you like to be my friend?" She said this as she pushed him, with her hand on his chest, onto his back. She mounted him.

"Would you like to be my friend?" she whispered in his ear again as he slid inside her, harder than he had ever been before, and before he had even realized he was hard at all.

"Would you like to be my friend?" she asked again, as she rode him. He tried to push back, to thrust upward, but she quickly overpowered him, smashing down on him sadistically, surrounding him with pleasure of an amount immeasurable.

She took him by the wrists with her hands, which were suddenly colder and harder than he recalled. She pinned his hands down above his head, and he did not fight. Could not resist even if he had wanted to. But why would he want to do a silly thing like that? Then she said, in her liquid magma voice that was melting his mind,

"Would you like to be my friend?"

And he said,

"Oh, God, yes! Raven, God, please. Yes!" Then a series of sounds that were not words.

She had been speaking into his ear, Her large breasts pressed against his chest. Skin to skin. She smelled like a burning match. Was nearly as hot as one.

The moment he had said his first 'yes', She had risen from him, smiled again, showing all of those pretty teeth. Those teeth parted. Her tongue slid out.

To him, it was beautifully black.

To him, it was wondrously long.

Ty rejoiced internally as he watched Her long, black serpentine tongue slide from between Her teeth and make its way across Her lips and down Her chin and unto him She sent this burden. This burden of a pleasure that he would never know again. Pleasure that he would, for the rest of his life, never match. He knew this, intrinsically, even as he was in the midst of that pleasure. He understood that he could never find it, never remake it again. He even knew, right now, that he couldn't completely capture it. Even in the moment, he couldn't fully appreciate the things that long, black tongue would do to him. And what he would do to Her, and what they would do to each other.

Death would be okay after an exchange such as theirs. Because, after such an exchange, life would always feel hollow, empty, devoid of something and many things. All of those things Her.

For the first time since he had been told that his father was never coming back home from the war, for the first time since realizing life was an unfair condition, Tybalt cried. Tybalt mourned.

He already missed Her although She was there on top of him. Around him. Even though he was there inside of Her. He wept.

She swept that tongue of Hers against his cheeks, suckling at his tears. Searing and burning his face in a way he so adored. He let Her, crying and laughing and tightrope walking across the thin line between manic and morose. Her tongue made its way into his ear.

An inch into it.

Deeper.

Licking, cleaning, tasting, invading him in a way he hadn't even considered could be so pleasurable. He went to grab Her, to hold onto Her, but the waves of pleasure emanating from his ear downward caused his body to do nothing but seize and shake. She rode him as he relinquished all control. He didn't want this to end.

"Let me be with you. Raven, please. Let me take care of you. I can be yours. I can be more than your friend."

Words such as these hadn't been uttered by Ty Ward since he was a nine-year-old proposing to his third-grade teacher on Valentine's Day. The subsequent embarrassment, and the talking-to he received from his mother, had taught him that feelings were overrated and only led to trouble. Here, he was okay with trouble if it came in the form of the raven-haired girl.

Her tongue, burning hot, left his ear. It slid its way back over his cheek and rested on his lips. Sizzling. He suckled at the tip of it, ignoring the heat, aware of the bitter taste of his own hot earwax, somehow made delicious because it was now mingled with Her.

She extracted Her tongue from him with a ***pop***. A fresh gale of tears left him as he mourned this removal.

"Please," he begged. He begged, "Please, give it back. *Please* don't leave me. I can't... I can't..."

With Her tongue still lolling out of Her mouth, black and coated in saliva, She spoke. The words came out clearly, but Her voice had changed somehow. There was a raspy quality to it, almost a buzzing, as She said,

"I will forever be by your side."

He came. Erupted. He felt himself falling backward, falling down, falling up.

Falling.

He felt himself released in a way that was an existential thing. He died, then lived again.

He came, which was really him going, going to places, seeing bewildering things and experiencing so much of all there is before he came back.

When he came back, he felt Her still on top of him. He smiled at that.

He opened his eyes, his smile vanishing instantly, transforming into a grimace, then a scowl, then whatever shape a mouth makes when it attempts to house a scream.

Her tongue, it pulsed.

Her tongue, it writhed.

Her tongue, it broke into thousands of pieces, each of which began to fly.

They hovered, a small black cloud of flying insects coming from the throat of the woman he still so desired. Tybalt released his scream, and the gnats no longer hovered.

They swarmed to Tybalt, entering his wide-open mouth, flying into his nostrils, crawling into his ears. They covered him, a blanket made of living, moving fabric.

The gnats did not cover his eyes, however. He was still looking at this beautiful woman and only now noticing just how red Her skin had been the entire time. How Her eyes were far *too* blue. Neon ice.

And within those eyes, he thought he saw more eyes. Faces. The twisted, writhing faces and bodies and hands of countless tortured souls.

Beyond the buzzing of the gnats, he almost thought he heard them scream.

He joined them. Despite the gnats that invaded his mouth, he could do nothing but yell and scream and mourn, because he saw that this woman, who he had just released his seed into, had a torso that was now bulging and widening in every direction.

It was then he noticed that those were hands pushing at Her from the inside, stretching Her skin, Her skin outlining their desperate fingers.

She continued to swell as what looked like a hundred hands pushed at the walls of Her torso. So many hands. All eager for him. Reaching for him. Wanting him.

The gnats continued to pour out of her throat.

They swarmed onto him, into him. Everywhere. They covered his face like a second squirming skin. One that tickled him horrifically and horribly, causing him to laugh, causing him to laugh and scream at once – the sound of a nightmare clown made up of your every fear.

She stood, dismounting him, and he felt his flaccid penis flop onto his thigh, wet and hot and sticky. Even now, as all of him was being invaded by countless flying insects, he lamented being away from Her.

He wanted to beg Her and plead with Her to not go too far. To not walk away.

They could work their way through this, he wanted to say.

Instead, he rolled off of the bed and fell to his knees, releasing beastly howls and clown-like chortles. Those sounds turned to gagging moans as the gnats crawled and flew and climbed further into his mouth. They were everywhere. They had coated his tongue, turning it into a pulsating, living black tube. They fell into his throat, down into his stomach. The gnats fluttered there. They clogged his ears, many of them tumbling out as more eager gnats attempted to storm their way in. His nostrils were packed with a thick, writhing black gauze of these creatures. He felt them, one by one, entering the hole at the tip of his penis, burrowing into his urethra.

Everywhere.

The last place they reached was his eyes. They had covered every inch of him save for his eyes because they wanted him to see Her, pregnant with souls in endless torment. Souls he knew he would join sooner than he had ever hoped.

Though Her torso had become a house of horrors, Her face remained stunning. Her lush hair had changed, however. What now framed Her face were the death-black wings of ravens. She was still beautiful.

So beautiful.

Except for when She smiled.

This was what She wanted him to see. She wanted him to see Her smile.

Her mouth stretched open, drooped low, the smile took up half of Her face. A gaping hole counterfeiting human expression.

She had no tongue. Not any longer.

What once had been Her tongue had now taken up residency on and in every available space of the body of Tybalt Ward. Except his eyes. And once again he hoped for blindness, for inside of Her he gleaned sheer madness. She smiled at him with Her half-open face, as if cherishing his realization. This was what She wanted him to see. This: sanity's end.

That smile said,

This is what you wanted.

That smile said,

You and I.

It reiterated,

Forever. And ever. And repeat.

And repeat.

MONDAYS

i.

The next time Tybalt woke, he saw God. Jesus, more specifically. Ripped and dying on the cross.

He was in the narthex of the cathedral, Tybalt was. On his back. A young man with the same features of a young woman he had recently been involved with before she had decided to kill herself hovered over him. His finger pointing.

Tybalt shook his head in an attempt to free his brain of the cobwebs that only unconsciousness can weave around it.

"I *said*! Get. The fuck. *Out*! Asshole!" And the young man went to strike Tybalt again, only this time his arm was caught from behind by the hulking Heath Carlton.

"He was unconscious when you said it the first time, Tim. I think he gets your point" Then, to Tybalt, "And as I mentioned before, Mr. Ward, no disrespect intended, but it would be best if you leave. You're upsetting the family." Tim twisted out of Heath's grasp and stormed into the church proper, saving one last glare for Tybalt before the doors closed behind him.

Tybalt, still shaken, stretched out his hand for Heath to take in order to help him up. Heath only continued to look overtop the extended hand, directly into his boss's eyes. Tybalt could feel his control over everything slipping. Even his control over his grasp of reality.

The dream he had just come out of was so vivid and real and frightening and lovely that this fiasco happening in front of him seemed like a piece of a disturbing nightmare. But Ty knew that it was real enough. He winced as a throbbing pain began in his head. This definitely felt real.

He had been punched in the face, not tackled, he realized. He had been blindsided and knocked out.

The shame inside of him rose, troubling him more than the pain he currently felt. He had been trained to constantly be alert. Mantra 33: *Always be on your guard.*

Yet he had let the confines of the church give him a false sense of security. A mistake he reminded himself to never make again.

Gingerly, embarrassed the whole time, he slowly struggled to his feet when he understood that Heath wouldn't be helping him up.

He didn't break eye-contact with Heath the entire while, not wanting to risk being attacked again while he was in a daze. Not wanting the younger man to believe that this unsteadiness was some indication of weakness from Tybalt.

"Understood." Tybalt finally responded. "I'll see you on Monday."

Heath only grunted in reply.

Tybalt turned, head held high, and exited the church.

ii.

Tybalt wouldn't see Heath the following Monday, two days from the day of Bethany Helmsley's funeral. But he didn't know this yet.

All he could focus on, at that moment, a few seconds after exiting the Church, was the disorientation he was experiencing, and the feeling of déjà vu which was piled on top of it. He'd been here before, he was certain of it. Been here and wondered where to go from here. He briefly considered walking, but it only took a few steps for him to understand that he wasn't going anywhere on foot.

Head hurting, he hobbled toward a nearby bench and sat down with an effort. He cradled his head in his hands and wondered if he had been concussed. It wouldn't have been the first time. Years of martial arts training and playing contact sports had resulted in more than his fair share of bumps, bruises and bell-ringers.

He leaned back against the bench as he reached into his jacket to retrieve his phone. He considered calling the driver who had been provided to him by The Fold, but decided it might be best not to. He didn't want to have to explain to the driver what had happened. He didn't want word getting back to Mr. Johjima. *Little hope of that*, he thought bitterly, knowing that it would only be a matter of minutes before the owner of the company found out about the events that had transpired at the funeral of one of his employees. The second suicide-related funeral in a month. *I'll explain to him that I was trying to smooth things over. Damage control. He'll understand. They recruited me to The Fold. He values what I can do for him. I'm important to this company.* He tried to talk himself back up to optimism. He whispered Mantra 1 to himself:

"Rock bottom is just another place to bounce back from." His voice, and the Mantra, felt hollow to him just then.

Tybalt ordered a driver through a rideshare application on his phone and waited, hoping that whoever straggled into or out of the church would leave him be. He couldn't recall the last time he had felt this embarrassed, this ashamed.

How could he allow himself to be blindsided like that? By a punk kid. And then to be dressed down by his underling in front of so many people...

He calculated.

He told himself that he would find a way to get even with the both of them. He would wait a while, but they would be made examples of. No one disrespected Tybalt Ward and got away with it.

His vehicle showed up, slowed down. A dark car of a make and of a model stopped nearly in front of him.

Tybalt confirmed both the make and model of the car with his phone. He looked around, glad to see no one was watching him, and, with vengeance still on his mind, he grimaced and gimped toward the car.

iii.

It wasn't until long after he had arrived home, with his anger subsided and his head cleared of the cobwebs, that Tybalt allowed himself to think of what had happened while he had been unconscious.

He considered the events at the Black Bird Bar and Grill something that *had happened* because they seemed, to him, as real as everything else that had happened that day. He recognized, rationally, that it had been a nightmare brought on by a brain-jarring sucker punch thrown by the last surviving member of the Helmsley family. But he couldn't shake the idea that it was something more. Some sign.

He tried to think it through, tried to consider the details, find a reason for why such things would have been on his mind. Why they might have entered his dreams.

The woman... he could only vaguely remember her now. In the haze of his memory she was a wave of unfathomable want and need. A red tide pulling him under. He felt for her the way he would imagine an addict feels for their drug of choice when edging toward the precipice of withdrawal.

He lay in bed, withdrawing, unsettled, overheated, wanting, craving, needing. But the more time that passed, the more the memories faded in the way dreams tend to, and the less certain he became of what it was that he was so in want of. What he knew for sure was that he felt he was devoid of something, that something was missing. Something was wrong.

Tybalt had always stuck to a strict sleep regimen. He followed the tenets of Sleep Hygiene: No coffee after 12 PM. No alcohol after dinner. He didn't look at any sort of electronic screen an hour before his bedtime, which was 11 PM nearly every night. He never took naps. His room was strictly for sleeping and for sex. Nothing else, no exceptions. He valued his sleep more than anything else. And here he was, not having any.

He rolled over and looked at his alarm clock. 1:25 AM. He used an old-fashioned digital device so that he wouldn't have to look at his phone between going to bed and after he had showered in the morning. He was a hard worker and knew the importance of getting the requisite amount of sleep needed to maintain optimal performance. If one incident threw off his routine, it could result in his day, and maybe even his week, falling sideways. This is why he stuck to his regimen, because his regimen made him consistent. Made him better.

He thought of his routines now. Hoping that thinking of the regularity of his habits would help him sleep.

His weekday routine was the same each and every morning. His first coffee would be ordered at approximately 8:20 AM in a Starbucks just outside of the Helping Hand office building. It was almost invariably a Caramel Macchiato. This first coffee would be consumed when he got to his desk three to five minutes later. Then he would begin his work day at 8:30 AM. An hour later, it would be yogurt and granola. Two hours after that, every morning, he would pour his second cup of coffee from the Keurig machine in the break room. It was never as good as the first, but it sufficed.

His was a life of structure, of discipline. Of control and great care. He was a dominator, after all. That was one of the things he thought to himself as he looked in the mirror each morning after his shower. He told himself it was another day for domination. For mastery. And one cannot go out and dominate the world without exercising complete control over one's self and one's own life.

The only true vice he allowed himself to indulge in was his proclivity towards fornication, particularly with women in submissive roles. He supposed that was a routine of his as well.

His mind drifted to Betts while insomnia shared his bed. Betts had been far from the first of his employees who he'd had his way with. But it wasn't a matter of sleeping with just his underlings, it was every subservient role: waitresses, secretaries, nurses, maids, any woman who made a living out of answering to others, catering to others, cleaning up after others, those were his types of women. The truly subservient women seemed to flock to him as well. He could detect vulnerabilities, interpret them. He knew exactly what to say and when to say it in order to get these women to do the things he wanted. He wasn't certain how the Tycoon had known all of this, but Mr. Johjima had made it clear that this talent of Tybalt's for seducing women who tended to follow orders well was exactly why he'd been recruited to begin with.

You're important to Johjima, Tybalt thought. *You've made yourself valuable, and you proved him right in the process.*

He had successfully Groomed and fully Involved one young woman into The Lifestyle – a term Johjima and Raynaud often used. The young woman had been a waitress at an all-day breakfast restaurant Tybalt had only entered for the purposes of seducing her. After she had flirted with him openly as she took his meal order, he had quite bluntly told her that she was too pretty to be a waitress. She had been offended by the comment, regarding him cordially but coolly when she came to gather his plate and leave his bill. She warmed considerably when she saw the tip he'd left for her. An amount it would have taken her weeks to amass. He had made sure to stay until she collected it, then told her to read the bill as he smiled and left the establishment.

On the bill was written 'Tip # 2: Meet me.' followed by the address of a hotel she could never afford to stay at, as well as a time for later that evening. A time she convinced herself she couldn't afford to miss.

Tybalt had changed the life of that young waitress, all on Mr. Johjima's coin, reaping many benefits for himself in the process. He took her places she had only hoped to see, promised her a world that had previously only existed in her fantasies. Then he had introduced her to powerful men, who had introduced her to other powerful men. And, just like that, she was Involved in The Lifestyle. The CEO had been thrilled, saying that it was incredibly rare for someone to have such a fast first successful Grooming. Tybalt had been on his way to potentially getting two other women Involved, and Johjima was aware of this. Had been proud of him. Things had been going so well.

And all while sacrificing my Saturdays to that suicidal bitch, Tybalt thought, angry again at the dead girl he blamed for the current state of his life. The girl he would always blame if things completely fell apart with Mr. Johjima and The Fold.

He punched his pillow in frustration. Yelled into the plush padding.

He felt like he was out of it. Control. Losing it.

Without it, there would be nothing left for him because that was what it had always been about. He had seen how society had controlled him based on his original name, based on the color of his skin, based on his age. Based on baseless things. He was frustratingly aware of the many things in the world he couldn't control, so he seized control of all he could. That feeling of controlling – of being in control, of the potential to control others – that feeling fueled him.

Yet here he was, not even able to control his own sleeping patterns.

Here he was, not able to stop his thoughts from racing, from going over every horrible thing that had happened in the last few weeks.

Here he was... worried. A word nearly foreign to him. Or at least it had been. Worse yet, he was uncertain. A term he had previously assigned to those with weak minds and even weaker resolve.

But here he was.

He thought of tomorrow. Sunday. The maid would arrive and he would get back some of his control. That helped to put his mind at ease, just barely.

He pressed his eyes shut.

There was tossing. There was turning. There were more tumultuous thoughts.

And, eventually, there was sleep.

iv.

Tybalt woke up feeling as though his sleep had been a blink. His head ached and his face hurt where he had been punched. His eyes burned. They were so dry he felt them scrape against his eyelids as he tried to blink himself into a state of full awareness.

He had dreamt of a bar. A real dive where the waitresses were topless and they all had the heads of ravens on their necks. He kept going from one raven-headed woman to the other, asking,

"Where is your mother?"

Saying,

"She said we could be friends."

Screaming,

"She said she'd never leave my side!"

Each and every one of them had initially only stared at him with black and death-filled eyes. Those eyes penetrated him and made his world warble. Distorting everything. They, each of them, opened their mouths to respond to him, but he could not understand a word they said because when they talked, they buzzed.

When they talked, they buzzed.

It was the buzzing that had driven Tybalt out of sleep and back to consciousness. Once he had risen from the nightmare fully, his now open eyes registered that there was a small fly upon his pillow.

That explains the buzzing, he thought as the dream began to fade and he was left feeling confused and hollow. He puffed out his cheeks and blew the fly away dramatically, watching it rise and weave through the air until it got far enough away that his eyes could no longer register it.

He would have to remember to pick up some bug spray on his way home.

Home from where? he questioned himself. And he tried to think of anywhere that was worth getting out of his bed for. He turned, rolled himself over until he was looking at the big red numbers on his alarm clock. It was 8:17 AM. Despite feeling as though he'd only momentarily dozed off, he had overslept by more than an hour, a rarity for him.

Sunday was his favorite day of the week. He would wake up (the rest of the day was, of course, contingent upon this) and make himself a bowl of granola and dried berries. He would then take a bath which usually lasted an hour, a time which he would split between a half-hour meditation session and reading a chapter of a motivational book. His current read, *Walk or Run, You'll Get There*, by Doctor M.R. Johnson (the Mantra Man himself) was presently on the counter in his bathroom, waiting for him. He was halfway through and had only been reading it for a week, which was a record pace for him. Tybalt was a notoriously slow reader, he would read things over twice or three times for fear he would remember them incorrectly even once. It was rare for a book to pull him out of his accustomed pace, though this book had done just that, quickened him. He had hoped he could incorporate some of the principles of the book into his office, bring his staff some motivation.

Motivation. He paused at the word as it crossed his mind now while he lay there in bed. Thinking about actually getting up and going through the motions of pouring granola and dried berries and milk into a bowl and chewing and chewing and chewing and forcing himself to swallow it down, and then dragging himself to sit in a tub of his own tepid filth while reading a book that he remembered being excited by, but now couldn't quite understand why, didn't make him feel much motivation at all.

Motivation. The word was a slur the way he thought of it just then. He thought of all of the things he'd had planned for that Sunday. That had been planned for every Sunday since the summit and his meeting with The Fold. He had hoped these would be his Sunday plans for the rest of a long and successful life. Now there was uncertainty.

Each Sunday after the meditation-reading-bath medley of an activity, he would typically engage in twenty minutes of yoga, followed by a jog around the neighborhood of at least five miles. He hadn't lied to Betts about Sundays being his day of rejuvenation, of mental and physical release.

The physical release was completed after he arrived home from his morning jog. His maid usually would be there working by the time he returned. This was the same young woman whom Bethany had had the misfortune of walking in on while she was providing Mr. Ward with said release.

She was of Asian descent, though he never bothered to ask her where in Asia she had descended from. He'd decided that he wanted her to be Japanese, as he had heard they were the most obedient of women. The most subservient. So, to him, that's what she was. During their initial meeting, the first time she had been in his apartment, the first time he had laid eyes upon her, he had placed five-hundred dollars in her hands and had explained to her the rules.

She had been referred to him by Raynaud Bedard, who had become his main connection within The Fold. This was one of the women Bedard had Groomed himself. And while she wasn't Tybalt's first, she eventually became his favorite. She had lived up to each of the requests Tybalt had made to Bedard. She was a cleaner first and foremost, not simply a prostitute. Functional *and* fuckable, that was what Tybalt had wanted upon making his request, sending in his order. She had to be more than someone who simply just lay there and was taken. Where was the dominance in that?

Tybalt had also requested, on the day he had called Bedard to make these arrangements, that along with being Asian and a cleaner, she had to have a high pain tolerance.

There had been a pause on the line. He would have thought he had been hung up on if not for the heavy breathing of the Frenchman in his ear. Tybalt had added, somewhat bashfully,

'Clamps. Paddles. Nothing crazy.'

'Oui, I comprehend. There can be no breaking of the skin. Understand?"

He and Bedard had agreed to only three other terms when it came to arrangements like this:

No frightening the girls.

No unsanitary behavior (unless agreed upon in advance).

Safe words, always.

Bedard hadn't told Tybalt much about himself. One of the few things he had disclosed was that he had been Grooming for over two decades. He liked to think of it as breaking them in, but never breaking them. The care of his Pets was of utmost importance, Bedard had stressed.

Pets. That was the word he had used.

Bedard had reminded Tybalt of all of this, reiterating the terms, not for the first time. Tybalt had listened, agreed vehemently, and hoped that he wouldn't be crossing any lines with some of the things he had in mind.

He knew that if he misplayed his hand – if his hands were too heavy – he would be out of the good graces of Bedard and their boss. Out of his graces, out of his offices, out of a new and wonderful lifestyle

Tybalt had placed five-hundred dollars in the hands of the Asian cleaner with the high pain tolerance when he had first met her in order to ensure that he would not be on the outs whatsoever. The five-hundred was a gratuity. Bedard paid the girl's salary, paid her well. But Tybalt wanted her to feel incentivised. He and the girl had discussed many incentives, and just what those incentives depended upon at length. Eventually, they had come to a verbal agreement as to how the cleaning arrangement – which is what Tybalt thought of it as – would go from then on. And, as if to prove that he meant what he had said about the importance of her household duties, on that first day he simply asked her to clean.

When she had begun to clean, he cleared his throat to gain her attention. She looked at him with a Swiffer in her hand and a bemused look on her face. He tilted his head and smirked at her until she understood. She smiled at him in response as she removed her clothes. The smile had been painted on. Shoddy art. He could tell it wasn't genuine, but he preferred that in some ways.

He had lowered his pants on that initial day of her duties, and put himself into his hand.

And on that first Sunday, he had only watched her clean.

On a later Sunday he would burst through the front door, returning from his jog in a sweaty huff, and she would be there, on his couch, with her legs open. And he would run between them. Then she would clean him in the shower.

On another Sunday he would nearly collapse into his apartment, exhausted, famished. She would be on the kitchen table. On her knees, bent over with all of her underparts presented to him. He would eat. And exhaust himself some more. Then she would clean him in the shower.

On some Sundays she would wait until he found her in the shower itself, but even on those days he wouldn't allow her to clean him until she'd had him dirty, sweating, smelly. There was something about having this maid, this person who was paid to make things clean, be with him while he was at his dirtiest that filled him with a wanting and a carnal greed that he didn't quite understand. Nor did he need to understand it in order to satiate it. It gave him the feeling of control, and that's all that mattered.

He took to calling her Sakura (after a character from the video game *Street Fighter* that he had always enjoyed in his youth), despite the fact that her name was Candace. She was only permitted to call him 'sir', when she wasn't regarding him as Mr. Ward, that is.

Laying there now, in his bed, Tybalt had all of these memories run through his mind in a flash. Sakura always made his Sundays better. The two had shared several months of memorable Sundays, which was why that day was his favorite of the week.

On this Sunday, with his schedule already destroyed, Tybalt thought about the effort involved with the process of granola and berries and a bath and a book and a woman who he knew nothing about other than her touch and taste and feel. He reached into the top drawer of his nightstand. Amidst the condoms, lubricants and sex toys, Tybalt grabbed his cell phone. He typed out a text message to Sakura. New instructions he never thought he would ask of her. New instructions he knew she would be more than happy to abide by. The message read,

"I won't be needing a cleaning for the time being, Sakura. I will give you further instructions when you need to know them. Stay clean for me. Don't worry, you'll still get your tip as promised."

He hit send, then threw his phone across the room onto a pile of dirty clothes he had left there for the plan he'd originally had in mind for Sakura. That had been before this malaise – whatever this was – had him feeling so out of sorts. The plan had been for her to wear a kimono and wait for him on his pile of dirty laundry. He had been so excited about that scenario, though now the idea of such a tryst seemed as if it would be more hassle than Hedon. Everything other than laying there felt like a hassle not worth the effort. Which is why he had thrown the phone, not angrily but matter-of-factly, as if that would be the last he would need of it for the day.

He thought that he heard it vibrate, perchance to challenge him, to test the man who couldn't resist opening an email right away lest he miss out on some crucial piece of information that would help him to get ahead of the game. The work game, the social game, the game of life. His was about seizing opportunity, and one doesn't seize opportunity by ignoring potentially important information. But, on this day, he only wanted to seize the opportunity to rest enough so that he wouldn't feel so terribly tired tomorrow. Monday.

He ignored the vibration he thought he had heard from his phone.

Rolling in the direction opposite his mobile device, he saw that the little fly was back on his pillow. He blew it away again and closed his eyes. He pulled his weighted blanket over his head in an effort to shield himself from the insect and from his phone and from the world.

For the first Sunday since he had suffered from a terrible bout of the flu during his senior year of high school, Ty Ward never left his bed.

V.

If you had asked him how he felt about Mondays, Tybalt Ward would have told you that he thought they got a bad rap. If you had asked him, on any Monday other than this particular Monday, how he felt about the first day of the work week, he would have told you that each Monday was a chance to reset and have a better week than the last. It was a chance to evaluate what you had done wrong the last week and put into practice the calculations of how to do better. In that sense, Mondays were the most important day of the week. The day you could routinely and reliably schedule a fresh start. Don't so many people do just that?

I'll start exercising on Monday.

I'll start my diet on Monday.

I'll put this new financial plan into action on Monday.

I'll work up the nerve to talk to that beautiful human being from my English class who is probably out of my league next Monday.

You've heard these. Said them.

Tybalt would have told you that most people hated Mondays because they couldn't handle the often unrealistic expectations that they put on that day. Couldn't handle the pressure that Mondays, through no fault of their own, seemed to attract.

But he could handle the pressure. He could and he loved it.

Ordinarily.

This was no ordinary Monday.

This was another in a series of days that all seemed to be out of his control. Days that seemed to plan for him rather than allow him to plan for them.

The first plan that this particular Monday had for him was to make it so he would do the inexplicable thing of sleeping through his alarm clock.

This, much like his spending his entire Sunday in bed, was a thing that had not occurred since High School. It hadn't occurred mainly because his alarm clock functioned as more of a precautionary measure than as an actual instrument he truly relied upon. He was usually awake before the sun. He took pride in this, as though he were in competition with the celestial body over who could consistently rise first. This gave him enough time to get in a hundred sit-ups and a hundred push-ups, check his email and catch up on the news, all before hopping in the shower.

He would leave his house at 8:00 AM each morning, and he would be at his desk, caramel macchiato in hand, twenty-five minutes later.

On this Monday he woke up with his clock displaying 8:26 AM, and the jolt of adrenaline that shot through him when he realized he would be late for work did him better than any cup of coffee ever could. He scrambled to get out of his bed, his weighted blanket seeming much heavier than it had ever been. He eventually got to his feet, stared accusingly at the clock on his nightstand, and wondered just how he could have slept through an alarm. He didn't even recall attempting to hit snooze. He stood for a moment next to the nightstand upon which the alarm clock sat and, for some irrational reason, thought to take the device, wrench it from the wall and throw it out of the window. This was an action that he would previously not have even considered, but somehow doing damage, any kind of damage, even though he knew logically that it would only cause him more stress in the very near future, seemed like it would be a source of great relief. He attempted to calculate, and was eventually able to talk himself out of this bit of cathartic destruction. Instead, he reached for the drawer beneath the clock, pulled it open, and looked for his phone.

It was gone.

A feeling of frustration began to rumble its way up from his bowels to his chest, threatening to turn into an explosion once reaching his mind. But by the time that frustration had gotten to his head and was about to tell his arms to tell his hands to grab the clock and hurl, he remembered that he had already thrown something.

His phone was in the laundry pile. He flushed even though no one was around to make light of his embarrassment. He thought of Mantra 6:

Do not allow the things which you cannot control to take control of you.

That's what he tried to remind himself as he scrambled, in a fashion that seemed quite out of control, toward the clothes in the corner.

Once he had found his phone, he mourned the morning even more. It had died at some point overnight and he didn't have time to charge it. He didn't have time for anything.

He grabbed the same shirt and pants he had worn to the funeral because they were right there in front of him. The clothes had picked up a bit of a musky odor from the truly dirty laundry they had lain upon for most of the weekend.

He didn't care.

If Tybalt hadn't been so frantic, he would have realized that this lack of caring should have been a troubling thing. He rarely repeated outfits in the same month, let alone days apart. And he wouldn't wear anything that wasn't freshly dry-cleaned or pressed. On this Monday, however, he simply put on the slightly damp, musky clothes from the pile upon which he had hoped to have sex with Sakura the maid just a day earlier.

Once dressed, he bolted out the front door, only stopping when he realized he hadn't locked it behind him. By the time he realized this, he was already twenty feet away, already more than halfway to the elevators. That was when the meticulous, careful, paranoid, regimented Tybalt Ward simply shrugged his shoulders and thought to himself that he suddenly didn't feel like he had much that he would consider truly valuable. If some mysterious stranger was waiting for him to leave his apartment in order to sneak in and rob him blind, then that stranger was welcome to whatever he wanted. Nothing in there felt very important just then.

There was only one thing that mattered, and that was getting to work as quickly as possible. He knew the drama surrounding the two suicides wasn't over. He knew everyone would still want answers. Change. Improvement. Reform. He could feel the control he had worked so hard to establish slipping from his grasp and wondered if he could calculate his way out of this. He felt a searing sense of doubt in his stomach. Doubt. A thing that had been foreign to him for years.

He walked down the hallway, into the elevator, barely acknowledging one of his neighbors who was walking out of it. He apologized noncommittally after his neighbor had to weave out of his way in order to avoid a shoulder-to-shoulder collision. Ty didn't even notice the glare from the usually friendly neighbor he thought of as The Nice Indian because people said hello and goodbye, nodded and forced smiles with their mouths, but rarely exchanged names in most neighboring situations.

When the elevator swallowed him and began to take him down to the main floor, Ty expelled a breath of stress and concern, he focused on it, hoping to inhale tranquility, resilience, faith. Things he may have taken for granted for a long time.

He was focusing on his breathing when the elevators opened to the building's lobby. The sight in front of him caused his breath to catch in his throat.

He looked at the ultra bright sun beaming in through the glass windows and doors that separated his lobby from the open air. It was too bright. He looked at the giant clock in the lobby hoping that it would read quarter to nine (he felt that it had only been roughly fifteen to twenty minutes since he had woken up in a panic). Instead, the clock read 11:15. It wouldn't be until later in the day that Tybalt would find out that there had been a power outage overnight, causing his digital clock to have stopped for over two hours. Right now, all he knew was that he was somehow half a day late. And fucked.

He couldn't focus on his breathing as he inhaled deeply, preparing to sprint what typically was a fifteen-minute walk to his office building.

He ran.

The next time he focused on his breathing it was only after having run so hard he felt he was running out of breath entirely.

vi.

By the time he arrived outside of his office building, Ty's clothing had gone from musty and slightly damp to smelly and wet. He had walked the last half a block to the building on the corner of River Street and Saltstone Avenue, through a downtown not unlike most downtowns: tall buildings, pungent odors, disconnected people in a rush to go nowhere truly important. Traffic.

It was the traffic, as well as the need to assuage the guilt brought on from working in a profession that made it so he would be sitting down for most of his days, that had made Ty decide he would walk to work each day. He was used to the distance from his apartment to his office and he was a runner, but he had never sprinted for such a measure while wearing dress shoes. He had a feeling that he wouldn't be jogging for a while with the way his feet hurt just then. His feet, however, were the least of his concerns.

It was almost lunch hour. Not only had he not reported for duty, but he had been unreachable for the entire morning. This was a week after one of his direct subordinates had killed herself. This was after a weekend which had included his being knocked unconscious by a sucker punch from the brother of his direct subordinate who had killed herself. At her funeral.

All of this was only one month after another subordinate had taken his life.

His superiors were going to ream him. Lube-less.

He didn't need to look down at his outfit to know that he looked a mess. He had adjusted to the smell of himself, but he knew it wasn't a smell that others would adjust to so easily.

For a heartbeat, he considered turning and walking back home. They would call it job abandonment if he just kept refusing to show up. But that wasn't the sort of man that he was. Especially when he had made such strides with Mr. Johjima and was closer than ever to being accepted as a full member of The Fold.

This wasn't just about a job, this was about status, this was about the promise for a future with much more than he or the idiots he had descended from could ever have hoped for. He thought of his father then, while he was forcing himself to walk slowly in an effort to cool off. As he was approaching his office building, approaching his fate, Tybalt thought of the last time he had seen his father.

For years the memory had always been filed in his mind under 'The Day Before He Went to War'. It had been an innocuous departure. A pat on the head followed by the words from a voice he no longer remembered saying, 'be good to your mom and sister'. He had cherished those words at the time. What he had found out later in life was that his father had made it a habit of leaving for long stretches, being a mule, doing extended shifts of security at one crack house or whorehouse or the like. Working his corners, occasionally being one of a crew of body men hired to accompany certain higher-ups in his gang when high stakes deals were to be made. That was his father's world. A world Tybalt despised.

Years later, when his mother had finally come clean, she had stated that his father had done it all for them. Her, Tyrone, Tanay. He had put food on the table for Tyrone and his sister, even if at times it was just barely.

Ty, at that point, spurning the final advice given to him by his dad, had told his mother that she should have met a man who could get a real job.

She had slapped him. It took a long time for him to stop feeling the sting of that blow. The longer it stung, the more difficult it became to continue to respect her.

His mother had gone on to tell him that his father had been arrested when he was only eighteen. Possession of marijuana, which equaled nearly a year of his young life in jail.

He never had a chance, she had told Ty. When he came out, he couldn't find an honest job, not one that would pay someone with a record anything above minimum wage. So, he did what he had to do, she had explained to Ty, her emotions pouring out of her eyes, leaking from her nose, distorting her voice. She had reminded Ty that his father had done it all for them.

All Ty had heard was that his father was a convict and a criminal; his mother, a liar and an enabler. And that was the blood that coursed through his veins.

Repulsed, he had walked away from his mother without a word. Without hugging and kissing her goodbye for the first time since he was old enough to perform such actions. What hurt him the most wasn't that she hadn't told him the truth, it was that she had gone so far with the lie. She could have made his father anything – a trucker, a fisherman, anything – but she had implanted into an impressionable boy that his father had died a hero. Tyrone had always pictured his father taking out a swath of the enemy, killing dozens while dying in a hail of bullets. Probably raising up a finger, pointing it to the sky and screaming, 'For America!', with his last breath.

The truth had not only killed that young boy's imaginings of his being the son of a great man, it had set the foundation for the hard man he would become. Their relationship had been strained since then, Ty's and his mother's. They spoke. He loved her, but he had never quite been able to respect her the same since he figured things out. The pain from her slap may have faded, but the truth still stung.

Ty thought of his father more often than he did his mother, even though his mother had been an active part of his life for over thrice the amount of years. He thought of his father every time he felt ashamed, that was a given. And he was feeling plenty ashamed just now, standing at the entryway of his office building.

He was about to step into a beartrap, hoping to limp away in one piece. If he had been better prepared, he would have made sure he was presentable, on time, showered, shaved. Not so fucking discombobulated.

But he was here, handling his responsibilities, holding his heavy head high. Tybalt made sure to always hold his head high. That was one of the few lessons of his father's he had held onto even after the truth was exposed. He hoped it would count for something today, and he hoped his stellar record with the company would speak volumes at a volume loud enough to drown out all of the terrible things he was certain had been said about him since the day Bethany had stormed out of this same office building he was currently gazing at. Panting onto.

He pulled in and exhaled two very deep, focused breaths, adjusted his clothes as much as he could, and proceeded to enter the building, feeling very much like an intruder in a place he had once dreamed of as his own.

vii.

"Mr. Ward?" This was the security guard who sat at the large glass desk in the lobby of the building. Ty knew the guard well enough, had made small talk with him from time to time about the Mariners or the Sea Hawks. Ty made it his business to make small talk and chit chat with most of the people in the building. He didn't enjoy it, but knew it was necessary for his reputation. For his brand.

He believed that the guard – Brad was his name – was hailing him in order to make conversation. Ty wondered briefly what he had missed in the sporting world over the last couple of days that he had spent mainly bedridden. There were two seasons in and around Seattle: Mariners season and Seahawk season. They were currently in the former of the two, and suddenly Ty couldn't think of anything that mattered less than a random game of baseball. This thought, on any other day, would have been a blaspheme, though on this day it was beginning to seem normal for him to just not care.

"Sorry, Brad. I'm very late for an important meeting so I can't talk right now. We'll catch up tomorrow!" Then, as he passed the large glass desk positioned beside a giant schematic of the building, framed and drilled into the lobby wall, Ty added, "Hopefully." and proceeded to speed walk toward the elevators.

He hadn't looked at Brad during the exchange, and so hadn't noticed that the tall blonde man had immediately picked up his phone and made a call directly after calling out to Ty. He hadn't looked at the panic on Brad's face as he waited for the elevator. Hadn't noticed the burly man rumble out from behind his desk and actually give slow-footed chase to Ty.

He hadn't noticed the guard until his hand had been placed on Ty's shoulder.

Aggressively.

On this occasion, there was no calculation, his reaction was instinctive. He turned and grabbed the security man's hand, putting him in a wrist lock, applying pressure in a way that made the guard bend to a knee.

Ty hadn't known it was Brad, he had been frazzled, on high alert. Preparing to defend himself verbally had somehow caused him to be on the defense in a physical way. And then he had felt the heavy, unexpected hand clamp down on him. He immediately released Brad's hand when he realized the mistake he had made.

"Brad... My God. I'm sorry, I thought... I thought... Well, I'm not sure what I thought, but you shocked me and I sort of just reacted. I'm... I'm sorry..."

Ty heard a ***ding!*** behind him. An elevator had arrived. He ignored the sound with a great deal of strength and restraint. He reminded himself that he was already nearly four hours late, another five minutes wouldn't make his case any worse. And, judging by the look of shock and reproachful dismay on Brad's face, Ty knew that there was a more immediate need for damage control down here.

He briefly imagined being hauled away by the police. The word 'assault' flashed across his mind like a headline immediately after the image of his arrest. Ty stammered a few more apologies, Brad had gotten back to both feet and was rubbing at his wrist where Ty had nearly popped it out of place. He took a step back, away from Ty. The look on his face was reminiscent of a puppy struck for the first time by an owner it hadn't known was capable of such an action.

"It's alright, Mr. Ward. I shouldn't have grabbed you like that."

Ty wished he had been recording those words, just in case the guard decided to change his tune at some point in the future and make a payday out of him. He wondered about what the cameras in the lobby would show, and felt they would illustrate that his reaction had been justified. And with that thought came a wave of relief. Though upon that wave of relief was a question that only then became apparent to Ty.

"Why *did* you grab me like that, Brad?"

Brad's jowls began to jiggle as words fought to make their way out from between his cheeks. His eyes bulged, his face made and expression that stated he had never expected to be asked why he had sprinted after this man and grabbed him so forcefully.

"You can't go upstairs." was what finally made its way out of his face. He took another step back, held his hand even more protectively against his bosom. Shrunk in a way that was not befitting of a man meant to guard security. Ty was disgusted. Such craven behavior had always rubbed him the wrong way. He went to respond, to tell this pathetic excuse for a man that 'can't' wasn't a word he could ever say to Mr. Tybalt Ward.

"All due respect, Brad. 'Can't' isn't a w–"

Ding!

This time the noise interrupted Ty. Cut him off mid-threat. Stopped him from speaking because he suddenly *knew*, as if he'd had a premonition that wasn't premonitory enough to make any use of.

He knew who he would see step out of that elevator. And he knew it would be a man who could tell Ty Ward 'can't' and 'no' and 'don't' and 'leave' and 'you're fired' and any number of statements Ty would find to be life-altering in a very negative way.

"Is everything okay here, Brad?" spoke an accented voice from behind Ty. The voice he had expected to hear.

"Yes, Mr. Johjima. I was just informing Mr. Wa– "

"That's enough, Brad. You've done well. Tybalt and I will speak alone."

Brad nodded and slunk away. Once again the sight of him reviled Ty. That revulsion was only topped by the terrible recognition that his boss had decided to address him by his first name in front of a subordinate, something that Ty couldn't recall him having done prior.

He finally turned to look at Mr. Henry Johjima, Japanese-American business Tycoon. Owner of Helping Hand Home and Auto Insurance. Owner of this entire building. Despite owning the building, he rarely ever made an in-person appearance there. Ty was certain that this wasn't a coincidence. Mr. Johjima was here because of him. Had driven or flown in from God-knows-where to address what he imagined they were calling 'the Ward Situation'. And Ty had kept this mogul, this man he modelled himself after, this billionaire, waiting.

Ty felt his stomach slowly turn upside down.

"Listen. Mr. Johjima. Sir..." Then he bowed. For some inane reason he decided that he would interrupt his apology, his necessary grovelling, to bow to the man as though he had just arrived here from Japan. The look on Mr. Johjima's face once Ty had stopped bowing and was face to face with him once again was one of confusion and pity.

Ty felt his bowels loosen in his upside-down stomach.

He proceeded to emit a rather unappealing surge of verbal diarrhea.

"...Mr. Johjima. I've been under a lot of stress lately, as you can imagine. I don't know what happened but something stopped my alarm from waking me up, and my phone was dead and because I've been so under stressed... I mean, under so much stress, I overslept and that's why I'm late. And I'm sorry if I'm not presentable, but I ran here, you see, I had to sprint because I was late because of my alarm clock situation and the..."

This went on for quite some time.

Mr. Johjima bore Ty's prattling with the patience of a Yogi. Ty was in a huff, sweating again by the time he was done with his rant. Mr. Johjima put his hand on Ty's shoulder with the compassion of a father worried about a son veering down the wrong path in life. Trying to correct his course.

"I understand, Tybalt. There have been many... unfortunate... incidents that have occurred here over the last several months, culminating in the unpleasantness that occurred at Ms. Helmsley's funeral."

Ty felt himself cave in the middle. Felt his shoulders slump, his arms go limp, his head hang. Only later would he realize that he must have looked as pathetic to Mr. Johjima as Brad the Security Guard had looked to him. He said nothing. Only listened for the inevitable.

Mr. Johjima continued, gently grasping Ty by the elbow and guiding him to a more discreet area of the lobby. They stood in a corner made by the wall and a stone embankment full of tropical flowers.

"It was... unwise for you to attend the funeral, Tybalt. Do you understand that?"

Ty nodded, still unable to look into the eyes of the mogul he had idolized even before he had started with the company.

"Do you see how that might cause the leadership to question your decision-making abilities in times of high stress?" This time he didn't wait for Ty to answer, to acknowledge, he continued on, recognizing that it was time for him to rip the bandage off. "There were discussions held this morning, discussions that you may have been a part of had you been here, or even reachable. But you were not, and this is what cemented our decision. You will go on leave effective immediately. Given your recent... state of being... we will not call it a suspension, we will call it disability leave. A Mental Health issue due to the obvious stress of having two of your subordinates take their lives during your time here..." Ty couldn't help but zero in on the words 'your time here'. They were said with a finality that contradicted the chance for rehabilitation the words that had preceded them indicated. "...You'll have to see a doctor in order to make this all legitimate. The appointment will be set up for you and you will receive correspondence in your email pertaining to the details of your appointment..."

This also went on for quite a while. Or at least it seemed to, to Ty.

He looked at his role model and noticed that a small fly had landed on the lapel of his royal blue blazer. Then another. The two gnats were all Ty could focus on, and he welcomed the distraction. The words coming out of Mr. Johjima's mouth had long since stopped being words and started being nonsensical noise. Nonsensical noise that signified his ruin.

He turned and walked toward the exit, not sure if Mr. Johjima was still giving him instructions, not caring either way. It all boiled down to one thing: he was no longer wanted there. Which meant that he was likely no longer welcome in The Fold.

It was almost too much to process, compute. Calculate.

The man who had renamed himself Tybalt wandered cluelessly out of the building, wondering just how, in such a short period of time, he had allowed his life to spiral so far out of control.

viii.

Ty exited the office with confusion smothering everything he had once been sure of. He knew the direction of home, but had no idea just where to go from here. He was down and essentially out. Out of a job, out of a shot at being invited permanently into The Fold, out on the street not knowing which direction to walk in. He let his feet take him again, not paying attention to where he was going.

He almost stepped on it before he noticed it.

He looked down. Jumped back.

A cat.

He thought for a moment that it was a black cat laying there on the sidewalk, but it wasn't until its black coat began to wriggle that Ty realized it was a cat covered in a layer of gnats.

They were swarming the corpse, leaving nearly none of the cat visible. The low droning sound they made threatened to turn Ty's mind upside down. He covered his ears, refusing to let it. He looked around, wondering why no one was doing anything about the cat cadaver and why no one else was reacting to this maddening drone.

Ty watched with his hands still at his ears, making the world a muffled place, as a large black bird almost the size of the cat swooped down from seemingly out of nowhere and landed near its head.

Ty retreated several paces but could not take his eyes off of what was going on in front of him.

The bird, unperturbed by the gathering of gnats feasting on the cat, waddled over to the fallen feline.

The gnats, unperturbed by the approaching bird, continued to behave like a coat that writhes, squirming all over the corpse. None of them dispersed as the bird first pecked at the cat's head, then forced its beak into the dead animal's mouth. It began to savagely tear out chunks of the cat's tongue, piece by pink piece.

Ty let out a low groan of disgust, took another step back, and narrowly avoided a collision. Two young women walked around him, each sparing him a reproachful look before walking directly over the bird and the dead cat on their way to a nearby hotdog vendor. The breeze created by their walking over the cat caused many of the gnats to fly off. Ty noticed then that there was a collection of gnats swarming, flying between the corpse of the cat and the hotdog vendor. More of the tiny flying insects were already at the hotdog stand. On it. Gnats were flying all over the station, crawling atop the vendor's wares. Yet he didn't react.

The two young women ordered a pair of sausages, Tybalt could hear them from where he was standing. He thought he heard the word 'weirdo' as one of them shot him an uncertain glance. He watched as the vendor grabbed two sausages, mindless of the roasted gnats that coated the tubes of meat, put them in buns and handed them to the women. They paid, then turned their attention towards the trays of condiments.

Even from this distance Ty could see them buzzing in there. Covering the banana peppers, peppering the onions. Hundreds of them, thousands maybe.

The women were about to open the condiment lids and be swarmed by them. Ty, more out of disgust than out of any heroic sentiment, screamed,

"No!" The two women stopped and looked at him. The hot dog vendor stopped and looked at him. Pedestrians who had been walking along stopped mid-stride and looked at him. His face burned with embarrassment.

"Bugs." he said, feebly. "Watch out." He pointed at the container with the banana peppers and the–

He nearly lost control of his legs, felt them wanting to fold. There were only banana peppers in the container. No flies. No bugs of any kind.

He looked to the pavement where the cat had been dead and covered in gnats.

There was a cat there, but it was pest-free and very much alive. It was just a mangy orange stray that must have learned to hang around the vendor for scraps.

From the corner of his eye, Ty could see a large black bird flying away. When he went to look at it head-on, he saw nothing but air.

He looked back to all of the people who had stopped to look at him. Their wanting to avoid having anything to do with the crazy man on the street caused them all to restart.

Ty, confused, was very certain that his fitful sleep, combined with the excess stress added to his life recently, had caused his mind to trick him. He needed to lay down. He had been outside too long.

Even though he didn't have to run, and the running hurt his feet, he ran back to his condo, wanting to get back to his bed as quickly as possible.

CRAWLING

Tybalt heard the front door open and barely reacted. He had a feeling it could be one of two people: his maid or his landlord, they each had a spare key. Perhaps he needed one of them to see him. To judge him. To shame him out of this... funk. These doldrums. This malaise.

And if it was some unknown other? Some thug, some armed robber, some murderer? Maybe that wouldn't be so bad either. Life just seemed so dull these days.

Ty was still in bed. This was a week and one day after the funeral. Sunday. Six days since he had been put on indefinite leave. Six days since he had left his apartment. Four days since he had received an email from Helping Hand pertaining to an appointment with a psychiatrist. One that would take place eight days from this day.

He had read the words 'Long Term Disability Documents' in the subject line of the email and had hurled his mobile device across the room. It hit the wall, hit the floor, remained there for two days.

It was an insult to him, the idea that somewhere along the line, on his personal record, it would show that he had taken some sort of disability leave. That he would be thought of as disabled, mentally ill, weak. He couldn't have his peers and superiors thinking he was one of these snowflakes.

Depression. He scoffed at the word. Scoffed into his pillowcase which hadn't been changed in well over a week but smelled as though it hadn't been changed in months. He turned it over, thankful for the cool against his stubbly cheek. It didn't smell as bad when it was cool.

He heard the person who had walked into his apartment taking slow steps through it, toward the room, and he changed his mind about wanting to be seen in this condition. The closer the person got, the more he wished they would go away. All he wanted was to embrace the coolness of his pillow.

"Mr. Ward?"

It was Sakura. Candace. Whatever. He had forgotten to remind her not to come, and he now very much wanted her to leave.

"Mr. Ward? Are you okay? I hadn't heard anything, and I know how you hate when you don't get your cleaning." She said this with a fake Japanese accent that shamed her, but he was paying her five-hundred dollars more per week than she was accustomed to, and she was willing to suffer the small indignities because of that.

She was flirting. Uncertainly. Not sure if something was wrong, or if this was another one of his sex games. She had never seen the place this way before, had never known it to smell this badly.

"Mr. Ward!" she said again, a little louder. Ty heard her again, and the fake Japanese accent reminded him of Mr. Johjima, causing his failures to wash over him anew.

"I'm in the bedroom! I haven't been feeling well! You can start cleaning out there!"

He heard her rummaging in his living area for a while, and he lay there, listening, wondering what to do next. Wondered what she was thinking of him, what she would expect.

He calculated.

He had to do it, even if he didn't feel the urge to the way he usually did. He had to make her think that this was an elaborate game. It was one thing for his employment record to show that he'd had to take a mental health leave, it was another for half the state of Washington to believe the same thing. His name was in the news. His name was all over social media. He knew all of this, and that was part of why he had been holed up in his apartment for a week. He was avoiding everything. Avoiding watching his very future erode in such a public, impersonal and heartless platform.

Social media. Social mob.

Despite it being so public, he tried to remind himself that it *was* heartless, it *was* impersonal. Those were the things he held onto during the few moments he allowed himself the belief that everything might somehow improve. Strangers would move on to the next bit of outrage, the next topic that trended. But if the people who knew him personally began to actually hear that he was breaking down, that he wasn't bouncing back from this terrible disgrace, that would truly be the end of him.

Social media he could handle when the time was right, but if he lost his social network... that would be too much even for him to deal with. Especially because it would ruin any chance he had remaining of getting into The Fold.

He thought of Raynaud Bedard, the Groomer and Handler for Sakura. Candace. Whatever. If word got back to him that Ty was suddenly a forlorn, snivelling wreck drowning in his own stench and mess despite having access to a cleaning company whenever he needed it, he would be deemed to be someone with a screw loose. No one wants to network with somebody who is rumored to be without all of their screws well fastened.

He would do it, he decided after listening to her clean for three quarters of an hour. He tried to think of the times they had done this sort of thing. When he had come to her after a hard run, sweating, emitting his brand of musk, and the pleasure he took in her licking his sweat, watching that sweat drip all over her face, her body.

He was trying to get himself geared up when she knocked on the door.

He reached into his top drawer and grabbed a piece of gum. Sweat-stench was one thing, bad breath was a no-go. He was already beyond the reasonable musk of someone who had just finished running. He would explain to her that there would be an especially large tip coming her way for putting in extra hard work this time. He would say that he wanted to test her limits, to see how far he could go in his imaginings with her. To see how filthy he could be with her. She might tell people that he was a kink, a fetishist, a pervert, but all of that was better than being thought of as weak. Disabled. Besides, he knew of the sexual proclivities of a few of the people in his network.

He'd had drinks, a time or two, with Bedard. The French Canadian became somewhat loose lipped with his liquor. When he had questioned Tybalt about his need for a cleaner, and Tybalt had expressed to him his reasoning for it. Dominance. Control. Raynaud had laughed and explained he was the opposite in the bedroom. He had used the Japanese word 'Tamakeri'.

Loosely translated: Ball busting.

Further translated: The guy liked it when young Asian girls kicked him really hard in the testicles. *Really* hard. He couldn't truly get off without that.

Tybalt had cringed upon hearing it, cringed every time he pictured it thereafter. Every time he imagined his connection, Bedard – his associate with the salt and pepper hair, and slightly overweight, middle aged body – naked and probably tied up, being kicked repeatedly with his defenseless testicles just hanging there, the sack around them doing its best impersonation of a punching bag, he cringed.

Still, there was worse. Bedard – without naming names – had told Ty of an associate inside The Fold who was into fecal matter. His idea of a perfect night was treating a woman to a huge dinner, preferably Indian, something spicy, something ethnic, followed by a laxative, and him being squatted over while he lay in his bathtub.

Tybalt had laughed (after cringing) at those stories then. Now he wondered what rumors were circulating about him, waiting to be poured out of bottles all around the state. He agonized about what people may have been discussing over drinks filled with Tybalt's secrets. He, the former Mr. Ward, the rising star that fell.

A knocking sound again. Sharp. Three quick bursts against the door breaking Ty out of his thoughts of perversions and proclivities.

Rap! Rap! Rap!

Bone on wood divided by skin to indicate she was here. That she was ready. Waiting for her orders.

"Come in," he said uncertainly. Then, trying to restore the confidence he could hear had flown from his voice, he repeated, "Come in!" louder, more authoritatively. "And close the door behind you. Don't let them in."

She came in. He watched her turn around and close the door with an urgency that would usually have turned him up a notch. She stood by the door waiting for instructions. She obeyed so well. He bit his lower lip at the sight of her.

She was wearing the Japanese schoolgirl outfit that he had bought specifically for her. The closest outfit he could find that matched the clothing of the character he had named her for. He had told her to wear it whenever she felt like it, as a surprise to him. But to make him wait for it so that he wouldn't know when to expect it. He was giving her a bit of control he knew he would mercilessly take back once she exercised it.

And here he was, surprised. Then disappointed. This wasn't how he'd thought he would feel upon seeing her like this.

She looked just like Sakura. Her blue miniskirt ended just below her crotch. She wore a crisp white schoolgirl's blouse with a yellow scarf around her neck, fashioned like a cravat. A white scarf was tied around her head like a headband, bangs sweeping over top of it. The rest of her hair was pulled back in a neat ponytail. On her feet were white socks protruding from clean, red high-top Classic Converse Chuck Taylor shoes. He knew they were clean because he had instructed her not to wear them there, but to change into them once she got inside his apartment. He was particularly careful about the type of filth he allowed into their dirty sex play. He wanted her filth and his filth, but nothing from the outside world.

He couldn't see under her skirt from his vantage, but he was certain that, under there, she either wore nothing or she wore the red boy shorts he had purchased for her. A part of him, deep down, wanted to see those boy shorts, wanted to have her take them off, turn them inside out and rub them all over his face. But a larger part of him wanted her to go. To just leave him be so that he could calculate and figure out exactly how he would get out of this rough patch. How he would get his name and his reputation back. How he could get back on the trajectory he had set to launch himself straight to the sky. That was more important than even Sakura-Candace in full Sakura garb. But he had to keep up appearances for the very sake of getting back his name and reputation and trajectory to the top.

"I've been out of it for the last few days. Bad migraines. I think what I need is a little relief. There's been so much pressure." Most of their role play started out in some generic, uninspired way. Improv was a strong suit for neither of them, but the words did what they were meant to do for Ty. The words were an exercise in control. And that's exactly what he needed just then.

"Clean up. Then come over here and relieve me. And don't you dare wash your hands."

"Yes sir." He watched her scurry into the large master bedroom. The illusion of maid and master was only broken by the expression on her face as she fully entered the room. Her nose wrinkling, her upper lip rising in abject disgust.

He hadn't changed his sheets in over a week, which typically wouldn't have been such an issue, but he also hadn't bathed or showered or done much other than lay in bed during that same time.

During that time he'd had several odd nightmares – each of which featured images of large black birds pecking at the eyes of a beautiful woman with blood-red skin.

The Red Lady walked down a road made of ice.

A road surrounded by bright blue fog.

The birds always rode upon her shoulders and her head, jabbing at her eyes, eating them out of her skull even as she walked. Even as she smiled a tongueless smile.

These images usually left him disoriented and drenched in nightmare sweat. The specifics didn't stay in his memory for long, fluttering away on the wings of those same ravenous black birds. But they left behind the feeling of something missing, something unsettled. They also left behind that unique stink that only nightmare sweat can create.

He hadn't bothered to change his sheets, even after such sweats. He would simply strip off his damp clothes and roll to a dry part of the bed. When those same clothes dried, he would put them back on. This cycle created what Sakura-Candace was describing to herself, in her head, as a deep funk. The smell nearly assaulted her as she got closer to the bed.

She decided to start cleaning as far away from him as possible. Hoping that by the time she approached the bed, and him in it, her nose would have adjusted to the stench.

He watched her clean.

She did the things she knew that he was looking for her to do. Bending over so that he could see that she was indeed wearing the red panties he had given to her. Sashaying instead of walking from spot to spot, making a real show of her duties. Making this cleaning session a performance. A tease.

Ty watched her, and this should have felt like Christmas, but it didn't. Not in a good way. It felt like unwrapping a present you've wanted for years, only to find that you've outgrown it the moment the present is revealed. He was unwrapping what he had expected would be a gift and finding only disillusion.

What this felt like was finding out that Santa Claus wasn't real.

"Enough. Come here." he said, again feigning the authoritative tone that had been so natural to him just a short while ago. He wanted to feel like a man again. He wanted to get whatever this was – this rough patch – out of the way.

"Crawl."

She crawled, taking note of the junk on the floor that she hadn't been able to clean in the short time he had given her. There were mostly bottles of water and containers of yogurt. She pushed through discarded tissue and, just as she was about to get to his bedside table and kneel the way he would want her to, she saw a large clear bottle, originally meant for orange juice. She thought for a second it had been mislabelled, assuming the container held apple juice within it, but she quickly understood that it was Mr. Ward's urine she was looking at in that orange juice container. She immediately took her eyes away from it and hoped he hadn't noticed that she had noticed the bottle. Again, she had to wonder just what was going on with Mr. Ward. He had a bathroom a few steps from his bed. She thought of that bathroom and hoped she wouldn't have to clean it. She had a strong feeling she wouldn't want to see whatever condition it was in.

The guest bathroom out in the hall hadn't been so bad. Nor had the living room or kitchen. They had mostly seemed neglected. Dishes were piled in the sink and on the counter, all of the trash baskets were in need of being changed, clothes had been strewn on the sofa, a light film of dust had begun to gather on several surfaces, and the fruits in the basket on the kitchen counter were decaying.

She had taken note of the traps he'd set out and had inspected for fruit flies or maggots. She had killed a couple of fruit flies and was thankful that had been all there was in terms of infestation. She had proceeded to toss the rotting pieces of fruit away and tie the garbage bag tightly around them.

What she had seen in the living area and kitchen had not been a fair precursor to what she had found upon opening the bedroom that Mr. Ward had always kept so neat and clean. He had pushed things at times, taking her to her boundaries, but had always been respectful when she would use their safe word or safe signal. She had always wondered if a guy with his sexual preferences – guys like Raynaud Bedard, the man who had originally given her this assignment, the man who she, just the night before, had punted in the testicles as he knelt against his bed with his back turned and his legs open – weren't just a little bit insane, teetering on the edge. How could they not be? What if this – she tried not to look at the urine bottle and the litter all over the usually pristine hardwood floor – was some sign that he had gone past a little insane and fallen into full blown crazy.

This was the first time she had ever remembered feeling scared around Mr. Ward. Frightened.

Still, she pushed on, convincing herself she was overreacting. She got to his side of the bed and knelt the way he had always told her to. Like a dog waiting for a treat. Those were his words.

She waited for more words from him now. Instructions.

Prayed he hadn't actually gone crazy. Hoped he wouldn't kill her.

He quickly removed the blanket from atop his body in a sweeping motion that she was certain he thought was sexy, but the smell that it revealed made her think that this was the attempted murder she had been scared of. Improv and acting may not have been her strong suit, but she held quite the poker face just then. She allowed the stench to kick her in the nose while barely flinching. Her eyes watered, but the rest of her face remained unperturbed. She tried to hold her breath, but the stench made its way into her system and was now kicking her in the stomach from the inside, making her feel like vomit might be added to her list of things to clean up. The man smelled like sentient filth. Functioning decay.

She held steady.

He shifted in the bed until he could hang his legs over the side, opening them as he did so. His crotch was facing her direction, and, despite it being covered by his pajama bottoms, from it came a wave of smelly reinforcements which began to lash out at Sakura-Candace's senses.

She held steady.

He shuffled his way to the edge of the bed where she awaited him. This the two had done several times before on Sundays past. He had tested her gag reflex previously, in other ways than he was doing now with his stench. She had always passed those tests. Now, however, as the stench whipped and lashed and kicked at her, she wondered if she was about to fail.

She held steady.

He inched out of his pajama pants and exposed the penis and testicles he knew he hadn't washed in over a week. She didn't know that fact, but, judging by the smell, she wouldn't have been surprised to have been informed of it. She hadn't thought a body that was still alive could smell so bad.

She was about to get up. About to shout an apology, promise to return his money, run out of the apartment and hope he got the help he needed, because nothing was worth putting something that smelled that way in her mouth. Nothing.

She was about to do all of that, but what he did next turned her expectations upside down. She was utterly shocked when he recoiled, then jumped out of the bed, his pants still around his ankles. He nearly ran over her in his efforts to run out of his pajama bottoms. He was out of them by the time he reached the foot of the bed. He shook each of his legs, looking down then looking up, then looking in a vacant sort of way at her.

Candace (Sakura to Ty) was certain he had gone mad. She thought about running again. Wondered if she would lose out on her standard pay from Raynaud if she decided to bolt. Wondered if that pay was worth any of this. And, just when she was about to run, about to say good riddance to a significant amount of money, Ty gave her an out.

"No!" he yelled. Then tried to control his voice and barely could, "You have to go. You have to get up and go. You didn't get them."

"Pardon, sir?"

"I guess you weren't able to get rid of them?" He asked it this time, trying to regain his composure, knowing that his last display had made him look like a fool and a coward. He could feel himself becoming disconnected from the inner circle. The membership into The Fold slipping out of his hands.

He would do damage control. Very expensive damage control. He would have to.

He could see uncertainty in her eyes. It wasn't just that she looked as though she didn't know what he was talking about, she had the look of a person who thought they may have been dealing with someone who had malfunctioned, someone who was confused. It was a look similar to the one he gave to raving derelicts when they raved too close to him for his liking.

"Were you?" he asked again, impatiently, ignoring the pitying look on her face. Not giving her a real chance to gather her thoughts, he elaborated, "Were you able to get the ones out there?"

"Sorry, Mr. Ward, but I'm not sure what you're talking about."

They looked at each other, both with bewilderment upon their faces. She, not knowing what it was that had spooked him, or what he was asking her about, or what the hell was going on here. And he, not knowing how she could possibly not be sure of what he was talking about. He stared her in the face, waiting for it to register there. But it didn't. And, after a long period of awkward silence, he finally gave up hope that she would say what was already obvious. Which is why he said,

"The gnats. The little flies. They've been all over the place and I just can't deal with them on my own. I'm not sure where they're coming from. Sorry you had to deal with that. They weren't part of the plan. I hadn't expected this next level of ours would leave me exposed to an... infestation." He still said all of the words that Tybalt Ward would have said, though, in this circumstance, given what had just happened, the words sounded light. Skimmed. Devoid of the confidence that Tybalt Ward usually had enough of to spare.

Candace wasn't sure if this was part of the game. She wasn't sure about any of this anymore. It was starting to become eerie. Uncomfortable. She thought of the state of Mr. Ward's kitchen.

There had been over a dozen homemade fly traps lying around, empty, pointless from what she could tell. These were bowls full of juices or thick, viscous substances covered by a layer of punctured saran wrap that she couldn't bring herself to look at for more than a glance. Along with these had been several burned-out mosquito coils. She hadn't known what to make of it all when she had seen it; she wasn't sure what to make of any of this now.

Not certain what else to say, she told him the truth,

"You're in luck, sir. I saw two fruit flies, and I killed them. I double checked after that, and there isn't a single bug out there. There was just a messy living room and a kitchen that was terribly neglected by a very dirty boy."

She had gone from speaking normally to turning on her fake Japanese accent halfway through that sentence. She wasn't sure if he was being sincere or if this was part of the show.

Ty hated that accent now. Would be glad to be rid of it. Of her. The times he had found her voice and accent to be so pleasurable seemed incredibly far removed from who and what he was at that moment. Those times seemed to have been a part of some past life. A life where he had a job and was a boss and he would have been ravaging the young woman in front of him right then and there.

Who was he now?

He wasn't sure. All he was certain of was that he had no desire for anything but solitude, and a solution to this problem that seemed to be getting worse and not better.

"No gnats?" he asked, bewildered, looking at her intently, wanting to make sure his eyes were seeing her correctly.

"No gnats. No insects. No infestations. Everything out there is straight and clean."

He observed her carefully, wondering if she was being serious.

She seemed to be.

He said,

"Okay."

He said,

"You can go now."

He told her that her services would no longer be needed, but that she should tell Raynaud that she was still coming here on Sundays for the next eight Sundays. He let her know he would pay her double – double her standard pay and double her usual tip – if she played along and told no one what she had seen here today. She responded by saying,

"Okay, sir. You have my word."

"And I have your pictures. And your video." Tybalt felt hollow as he espoused this threat, but he had to keep up appearances, had to make sure none of this got out there. The photos and video were part of her contract with The Fold, this much he knew. They were evidence to assure discretion. And more.

"Yes sir. You no have to worry, sir." They both wanted her to leave very badly.

He nodded. She bowed.

"Thank you for everything," was the last thing he said to her.

He watched her intently, waiting for her to break character. Wondering how she could keep it so straight – her face that is – with all of those gnats crawling all over it.

REORIENTATION

i.

"First of all, I'm very glad you've come to see me, Mr. Ward. When I was informed about your situation by Mr. Johjima, I made it a priority to clear a spot on my calendar to see you. And when you didn't show up for your first scheduled appointment, I was very concerned."

This was Dr. Sundra Lucroy. She spoke in a Scandinavian accent that Ty couldn't precisely place, other than to say it came from somewhere in Scandinavia.

He sat across from her and very much wished that she would stop yammering.

This was the third time he had left his house since he'd been told he had to go on this disability farce. The initial two times he had gone out he had done so out of absolute necessity. On the first occasion he had run out of yogurt, and he didn't feel like eating much else. He wound up buying a month's worth from the corner store, knowing that he was paying an arm and a leg for something he could have gotten much cheaper at the grocery store just two miles down the road. But he hadn't wanted to go there. He hadn't wanted to venture that far out. The further away from his home he went, the further he would have to run back if they decided to chase him. *Them.*

The psychiatrist's office was a distance that Ty would usually have walked to, and back from, but that was far too much open air. They existed in that air.

Them.

He had sprinted to the vehicle that had been waiting outside of his building to take him to this appointment. Once he was satisfied that none of *Them* had followed him into the vehicle, he'd tucked the small canister of bug spray he had brought with him into the pocket of his jacket. He caught a glimpse of the driver in the rear-view mirror, looking at Ty like he was a crazy person. It was the same expression that Sakura-Candace had directed towards him.

Same expression, different face. He had to wonder if he would live the rest of his life seeing that same expression on every different face that saw him for the first time. Or the second time. Or every time. He tried to ignore it.

He was in the process of making sure that same expression didn't appear on his face as he looked at the Head Shrinker in front of him. The psychiatrist, Dr. Sundra Lucroy.

She was a burly woman whose physical prime appeared to be at least a decade behind her. She wore a red skirt and white shirt beneath an old-fashioned red blazer. The blazer had thick shoulder pads built into it that reminded him of football Sundays. She had a pouffe of yellow-orange hair that Ty thought must have been a wig. He didn't want to imagine what she looked like beneath that wig. He briefly wondered if this was one of those transitioning people. Going from man to woman. He didn't understand it. But it wasn't his business to understand, he reminded himself. He was there to get a prescription and get back to work.

He was going through the motions, jumping through the requisite hoops that Mr. Johjima had set out for him. He had skipped his original appointment and had subsequently received a very to-the-point email from Mr. Johjima himself insisting that he abide by the therapy sessions. Telling him they were essential for his mental health, and that the sessions were a prerequisite to him returning to work. The email said to consider these sessions as his reorientation. He had to do exactly what was asked of him if he truly wanted to show that he was a Helping Hand man after all.

Here he was, doing what he needed to do, looking at this overweight and over-the-hill woman he wouldn't have touched had he been paid to touch her.

As she talked, he noted the lines that ran from her lips and eyes and burrowed into the rest of her face. Laugh lines, character lines, crow's feet. Her face was an illustration of a life that had been long lived. Ty wondered what she could tell him that would help him in the here and now. What advice he could take from a woman whose time had come and gone.

He noted that her makeup looked like it had been spackled on to hide those aforementioned lines.

He noted that her lipstick more surrounded her lips than it covered them.

Noted that her teeth weren't discolored, but they were crooked.

He observed all of these things and was thankful that she was so unattractive. He didn't want to think of sex or domination. He only wanted to have a frank conversation about a medication that would give him a boost, bring him back to optimal. He didn't need flirtations getting in his way. This was the next best thing to sitting across from a man.

"My apologies, Ms. Lucro–"

"Doctor."

"Yes. Doctor." For a moment before he continued, he was distracted by a glint of light reflecting off of some precious metal on the woman's ring finger. He paused to consider what the unlucky fellow who had stitched the name of Lucroy to this woman must have looked like. If there was such a fellow, he had Tybalt's sympathies. "I apologize for my absence. I've just had a bit of difficulty leaving my house these days. Bug season and all." He gestured vaguely to the walls of the office. Mrs. Lucroy followed the gesture, not certain what he was referring to. She allowed him to continue, "As I'm sure you've been told, it's been a trying time for me."

He had been trying to get out of this appointment for some time. Had hoped he could skip the shrink and just do the things he felt he needed to do to ready himself to go back to his office and sell more insurance policies than he ever had before. But it turned out that his word on being ready wouldn't be good enough. This unsightly doctor had to give him the *A-Okay*. The *Good-to-go*. Her word would determine how his future turned out.

Ty found himself out of control once more.

"My mother always used to say that trying times create *trying* times. This is a time for you to try your hardest to turn things around. This is your first step, and it's a big one. You should commend yourself for coming in, Mr. Ward."

He looked at her with barely disguised disgust. Her, sitting there with her bright red lips and her powder cake face, this shrink, this quack, sitting there quacking away. Judging him. Stealing money from God knows how many people for God knows how many years. Selling lies and peddling drugs. It was the drugs he was interested in. She could save her words for someone else. He was there to make the best of a bad situation. Mantra 20:

No matter what situation you are in, make it advantageous.

With this in mind, he understood he would have to suffer through this sympathy session (as he called all forms of therapy that weren't electro-shock) in order to get drugs from her. He needed something to help him sleep. Something to suppress his dreams while he did so. He'd heard they had those now – pills that tame nightmares. That was what he needed most. He often dreamt of dark things. Things that leeched the color from his days when he awoke.

He would want some uppers. Something he could slip into his two coffees per morning that would really get him going again. Just until he got the energy back to get going on his own. He wondered, not for the first time, if perhaps he should have been seeing a medical doctor and not this charlatan. Maybe he was having legitimate health troubles. But he wouldn't have known what to tell a medical doctor that would differ from what he was in the middle of telling this person.

"… and I don't think it's really all of the big deal the company has made it out to be. It's really just a matter of me feeling lethargic lately. I've been having these nightmares, and they've been keeping me up at night, and that's been impacting me in the day. You see I'm really a schedule-oriented person, so it's just a matter of me needing a few things to get me back on my schedule. You understand?"

"Yes. I understand." She looked at him carefully, and then began to scribble something down on the notepad she had in front of her. Ty hated that. Hated her having a record of everything. And who knew how she would twist what he had been saying. Make him seem like some sort of a softie. Some snowflake. He needed legal drugs to regulate his life, his schedule, his trajectory. That was all.

Not for a second did Ty consider purchasing illegal narcotics. Since he had learned of his fallen father's forays, he treated all illegal drugs like a personal enemy.

"It's really no big deal," he added as she finished scrawling on her notepad.

"Well I think you should be taking this quite seriously, Mr. Ward. I understand that we have only just met this once, but based on what I have been told, from what I have observed, your responses so far, and the questionnaire that you filled out up front before you entered my office today, you have very severe mental health issues."

"Pardon me?" Ty refused to believe this. Would not hear it.

"This is no surprise, Mr. Ward, considering everything that you have been through recently. And it is nothing to be ashamed of. You are showing the same signs of anyone who has undergone much severe trauma in a short period of time, Mr. Ward. There were deaths, there was a leave from your job. That is a lot to deal with."

"I'm fine. I'm just stressed. I'm jus–"

"Yes, you are stressed." She decided that she needed to take a more direct approach. She needed to get through to him the severity of his situation. "You are exhibiting signs of Post Traumatic Stress Disorder, as a fact."

"What?"

"Severe Depression. Agoraphobia."

"What?"

"Social and General Anxiety Disorders."

"What?"

"Psychosis. Schizotypal Personality Disorder."

"What the fuck are you talking about? What language are you speaking? I'm here because I'm stressed and I would like some pills that will make me less stressed. Also, if I don't come here, I won't be able to get my job back. It's a requirement of the... disability program." He nearly choked on the word 'disability'. The idea that he could be thought of as some mental cripple made him sick to his stomach. But he had to do this. Had to set right his trajectory.

She continued to babble on, and what he thought of again was his father.

Turf war or genuine war, it didn't really much matter, Ty was allowing himself to realize then, he had lost his father to a war. If he could survive that, he could survive anything. His reality had always been a bleak one, and he had always overcome.

The quack in front of him quacked out her quackery. None of it mattered to Ty because he didn't believe in the excuse of mental illness. To Ty, the world was made up of two kinds of people: those who could handle things, and those who could not. The only mental illness he believed in was the scourge of mental weakness. Quacks like Lucroy only enabled the mentally weak, never allowing them to strengthen. He refused to be counted among their ranks.

"...In short, what I'm talking about, Mr. Ward – and I would caution you about the language that you direct toward me in my office – is the opportunity for you to continue to heal instead of progressively get worse."

The two sat and stared at one another for a minute that felt like ten. Tybalt wondered if her face was hot beneath all of that spackle. Wondered what would happen if the sweat and spackle combined.

They were having a staring match. Two adults being two children, both wanting to establish an animalistic dominance. Ty could have continued the staring contest for a day or more, but he knew this wouldn't help him regain his status. They wanted him to comply, to show contrition, to show improvement. He recalled Mantra 27:

Unnecessary conflict is counterproductive.

And Mantra 31:

Don't let your pride lead to punishment.

"I apologize about the swearing," Ty grumbled as he thought of Mantra 16:

Never apologize unless not apologizing costs you something.

This was one of the rules he was most ardent about, and he knew it was a philosophy he shared with Mr. Johjima. Which is why he shrank in his seat as he watched the shrink scribble on her pad, knowing in his heart that she would inform his employer of this apology. He hadn't wanted to apologize. He had wanted to swear at the woman in front of him some more, but whatever she jotted down would be on his record forever. Would determine the way his life went from this point on.

Her pen, her pad, her word. Control.

"It's not so much the swearing, Mr. Ward, it's the swearing *at* me." She paused, leaned back in her chair, stared at Ty overtop her rimless glasses. "I've actually always thought fuck was a great way to release one's aggressions in a healthy and wholesome way... Fuck." she said, using the last word as a punctuation, using her entire mouth to slowly let it out. Shaping the word. Again,

"Fuck."

"What?"

"Stand up, Mr. Ward."

He didn't stand up. In fact, he somehow sat down further. He was a lump in the seat across from her, just staring. He didn't know what she was quacking on about, but he wasn't about to stand. He didn't see what that had to do with therapy.

Then he saw her look at him dismissively and take her pen and take her pad and move the two together in order to write ruinous things about him.

"No!" He stood. He had to follow orders. He couldn't have any other negative details in his record.

"No?"

"Yes! Yes... I'm standing, I'm standing. What were you going to write about me?"

"Important things, Mr. Ward. Can I call you Tybalt? Tybalt, in this notebook I enter the important things that let your employer know whether or not you are seriously ill and entitled to money, or whether you are faking it, being obstinate, and entitled to nothing. That is what this book is for, Tybalt. This book will help me to write my final report when all is said and done. That report will determine whether you will ever work for Helping Hand again. Perhaps whether you will be able to work in this field again."

She hadn't waited for him to give her permission to call him by his first name before she had done so, which was a matter that riled him. Who was she to be so disrespectful? This ancient, overweight duck. This overpaid talking Pinterest page.

He opened his mouth to say all of that, to tell her what he thought of her, but then the words from his brain reached the filter between their source and his mouth, and during that conversion time Ty got to calculating and calculating. The computations showed that if he called her an ancient overweight duck, he would be out on his ass, remaining in a rough and barren patch devoid of the greenery he was essentially being offered by Mr. Henry Johjima by way of Dr. Sundra Lucroy. With them was the prospect of growth, without them was desolation.

His thoughts came out of his mouth, through the filter, filtered.

"There's no need for that notebook anymore, Ms. Lucr–"

"Doctor." she said, her face so full of I-am-better-than-you.

"Doctor Lucroy... I don't think there is a need for that notebook. I'm on board. Please be patient with me, I'm not... used to being... disabled." The word was a blockage in the passageway of his throat. It had to be forced out. Given the Heimlich. It was Ambition that stood behind Ty, performing the career saving maneuver.

"Does that mean you're ready to follow instructions?" She said this in a tone and with an expression that he instantly recognized but didn't know why. All he knew was that it was a tone which demanded an immediate response, lest there be repercussions.

"Yes, Doctor Lucroy."

"Good boy. Walk over to this side of the desk, then heel."

His body visibly shuddered as a typhoon of dissonance stirred in his mind.

His mind was telling him to have some composure, some pride, to walk out.

His mind was telling him to do as he was told. Hers was a body, his was a body, he would just be doing the things that bodies were meant to do.

His mind was fighting itself. His body wasn't certain of what to do. And when it seemed as if he would stand there shuddering for too long a time for Dr. Lucroy's liking, she decided for him.

"There are photos... and video. Of you and Candace. And others."

Of course, he thought, a shiver of rage trickling down his body. He lamented giving the maid so much money. They had him by the balls, literally as it would soon turn out. They had information on him. Pictures and video of things deemed not quite acceptable to most members of society. Evidence to assure discretion. And more...

In the end, Ty ignored his mind and listened to the only voice outside of his body.

He did as she asked, walked around the desk.

He went to his knees a few feet from Dr. Lucroy. A few feet from her feet.

Still leaning back in her seat, she hiked her skirt up to her hips, opened her legs. For a moment Ty thought he saw a flash of brown panties, but quickly realized it was a thatch of pubic hair. He hadn't actually ever seen pubic hair that thick in person. He believed it was a thing that only existed in the porn he used to watch as a kid. Porn he had found clever ways of sneaking out of his grandfather's collection whenever he'd had the chance. Since then, he had only witnessed all of the beauty that waxing and shaving and trimming had brought to the world over the last several decades.

Ty wasn't a fan of retro acts.

"I'm not sure I understand what's going on here." He understood very well what was going on here. This was a power move. This had never been about therapy. This whole thing had been about punishment from the start. Mr. Johjima had entrusted Ty with a great deal of responsibility, a great deal of power, and Ty had abused it. Ty had brought shame upon the organization of a proud man. A proud man with true power. A proud and powerful man who believed in discipline just as much as Ty himself did. This was that discipline. This was a reestablishment of order. Of putting Ty back in his place.

Control.

This was Mr. Johjima putting his cock in Ty's mouth without needing to unzip his fly.

Ty looked at the thick covering of hair between this woman's sagging thigh flesh. He thought for a moment that he saw movement there, maybe something wriggling through it. He closed his eyes and convinced himself that it was just his imagination.

All of the stress. All of the stress.

"You understand exactly what is going on," Dr. Sundra Lucroy said to a shuddering Ty. This was not a question. She did not look for any sort of acknowledgement or acceptance or answer from Ty. His being on his knees was answer enough.

She said,

"Crawl."

He crawled.

She said,

"Eat."

He did that too.

ii.

Therapy continued on with Dr. Sundra Lucroy. Each session followed the same format with slight adjustments every time. Once she had felt sufficiently released of her aggressions in what she deemed to be a healthy and wholesome way, she went back to shrinking, to psychologizing Ty.

On this day, Ty was listening to her quacking away as if nothing had just happened. As if his head hadn't just been burrowed between her great, heaping thighs. As if he hadn't used the tissue paper from her desk to wipe her pleasure from his face after she had been done with him. The hand sanitizer he had smeared all over the bottom half of his face was to make sure nothing of her remained there. It burned in a way that he longed for after having to do *that*.

How could she be sitting there yapping to him about medication and therapy methods after she had just traumatized him in a way that made him possibly believe some of the quack that she was quacking? How could she–

It was then he remembered all of the times he'd had a subordinate relieve him of his aggressions in a wholesome and healthy way. Hadn't he had an underling blow him on occasion right before he went into some nuisance meeting full of insurance jargon? He recalled trysts with this sales broker or the next, asking one or the other to meet him at the office an hour before anyone else would show up. A very productive hour each time. Work, after mornings like those, was far less stressful. Didn't he use sex with his subordinates as a way to give himself a break or a boost throughout his workday? Yes. And yes. He worked them, they worked him. Then he sent them back to work, and he would do the same. He supposed that Dr. Lucroy was no different. He reflected further on the sales brokers he'd had in his office, Bethany Helmsley being among the most recent of them.

Bethany, breathing all sexily for him on that Goddamned bus. Bethany, with her willingness and eagerness to please. Bethany, on so many lunch breaks.

Fucking Betts.

Fucking Betts...

Not for the first time since her life had ended and his life had collapsed, he was angry with her. Truly angry. If only she had been strong enough to just deal, he wouldn't be dealing with all of this.

He sat bitterly in his chair, reflecting, enraged, the bottom half of his face stinging from the sanitizer he'd smeared there. The shrink talked, Ty barely listened. He was preoccupied with thoughts of all that he intended to do to her once he got back on his feet and out from under her thumb.

iii.

"Mr. Johjima, please. I've been to four of these sessions and I don't see how they're benefiting me. I get the point, I've learned my lesson. I'm ready to come back to work. Back into The Fold. *Please*, Mr. Johjima." Ty sat on the end of his bed hours after his fourth session with Dr. Sundra Lucroy. He was in a room that was dark but for the light from the lamp on his nightstand. With one hand, he held his phone to his ear. With the other, he held his stomach, some symbolic way of untying the knots that were entangling there. Mr. Johjima did not seem thrilled about being called outside of work hours. On his very private line. By someone he had already given clear instructions to. Instructions that were the exact opposite of what Ty was doing at this very moment.

"You have just said *please* twice to me. *Twice*. Since when do we beg? *We* are the Helping Hand, we never reach out for it. You are not where you need to be, Tybalt. Not according to Doctor Lucroy. She has recommended at least eight more sessions. She says she believes she can really get to the root of things. Open you up and make you a better man again."

Ty tried to imagine eight more sessions with Dr. Sundra Lucroy, tried to weigh whether or not accumulating the memories that would come from eight more experiences with her would be worth getting his old life back. He could live without the job, he had decided during his time off. What he regretted most was losing out on the opportunity to gain full access to all that Helping Hand could provide him. He had been on the precipice of the inner circle. Close to not only being associated with, but fully accepted into The Fold. He wanted that more than anything. To use his helping hands in order to take whatever he desired. Those in The Fold were the types of people who helped each other help themselves to many things.

They helped themselves to young ladies like Sakura-Candace. They helped themselves to exclusive shows, to parties of a sort that no one truly knew existed, to vacation destinations not located on any map. They helped themselves to all of the things that money and connections could afford. Tybalt had been granted a bit of access, a glimpse into that world. The Lifestyle. But he had not been let all the way in.

What he had heard about The Fold was hard to believe, but not unbelievable. It bordered on the conspiratorial. But conspiracies are only conspiracies until they're proven true. What he wanted more than anything was to see it all, to experience it all.

Those within the inner sanctum of this powerful social network were rumored to have cures. For what? No one he had heard this from was quite certain, but they were said to have access to things that kept the members young, rejuvenated. Mr. Johjima himself was into his eighties, yet he didn't look a day over sixty to Tybalt.

Ty wanted it all. He had been so close. And now some gay guy and his emo sidekick killing themselves had come down on his life like the heel of a boot, sending him back down the rungs of the ladder to success he had been so effectively climbing. The heel of that boot had crunched down on his hands and sent him sprawling into a pit so black he wondered if he would ever find his way out of it. If he would ever regain the bright optimism that had previously never seemed capable of waning. He wanted to get back up and jump on that ladder. Climb back to where he had been. Then past that point. But if that meant he would have to continue to crawl around for that hairy-crotched sasquatch of a quack, then maybe he had better start adjusting to the dark.

"Mr. Johjima, *please*. Doctor Lucroy... She is... I can't. The smell..."

"I believe in her methods, Tybalt. Eight more sessions with Doctor Lucroy is all it will take for you to regain your standing. This isn't too much to ask given all the damage done under your watch, is it?" Ty could say nothing to that.

Under Ty's watch, employees had quit after complaining of a toxic work environment. Thousands of people around the country had cancelled their policies after all of the social media backlash involving the two suicides, taking their insurance elsewhere. Many of these defecting clients stated they couldn't trust that their business would be handled fairly by a company that didn't value the lives of its employees.

There were many financial losses.

These losses were all bearable for a company with a profit margin the size of Helping Hand's, but they were losses nonetheless, preventable ones at that. Mr. Johjima loathed nothing more than preventable losses. That and bad publicity were atop the list of things he hated. Tybalt Ward had brought him both.

Ty stayed quiet, knowing that there would be no room for negotiation here. He was pushing things already. After trying the phone number on the business card Mr. Johjima had provided Ty with all those months ago at the Summit, Ty had called every Helping Hand office around the country in and effort to reach the CEO. When that had failed, he was able to obtain Mr. Johjima's personal cell phone number by pleading with Raynaud Bedard.

Mr. Johjima was right, Ty had been doing a lot of begging lately. That would change once all of this was over with, he told himself. He would never slip up again.

"Is there anything else?" Mr. Johjima fumed through the phone. When Ty didn't answer, he continued, "Good. You will be contacted by Dagny Cole from Human Resources if anything changes or once you have completed your sessions and been given approval by Doctor Lucroy. Ms. Cole seemed particularly grateful when she was told about your situation." The tycoon scoffed through the phone at Ty, indicating that he knew about Ty's encounters with Dagny. Ty didn't know how this could get any worse.

"And Tybalt?" Mr. Johjima went on, "Do not ever call my personal line again." Then the line went dead. Ty sat there for a long while, his phone nestled between his shoulder and the side of his face. He couldn't imagine himself moving, not even to put his phone away.

When the phone rang directly into his ear he jolted up, nearly jumping right out of bed. The phone banged against the ground, still ringing. He looked at it like it was an explosive device that might detonate the moment he went to pick it up, but he couldn't risk missing any important calls. Couldn't risk seeming like he was unreachable again. Unreliable. He scrambled for the phone, saw that it was actually a person he wouldn't mind speaking to. He managed to answer it before it went to voicemail, which seemed like a small miracle to Ty just then.

"Bonjour, Raynaud," Ty said, without his usual flair or charm. The greeting was a perfunctory thing.

"Hello, Tybalt," the Frenchman replied coldly. "I should cut short to the point. I have unfortunate news. For you." Tybalt didn't want to deal with more unfortunate news. His life, every day it seemed, was unfortunate news. He couldn't even bring himself to ask his connection what the bad news was.

When the Frenchman realized he wasn't going to be prodded, he went straight to it.

"I have had discussions with Candace recently."

"Who?"

"The cleaning woman. Petite Asian girl."

"Oh. Sakura." *That bitch.* "Yes. What about her?"

"We. You and me and her, we all discussed no frightening. She said you behaved frightening. She said that you practiced... unsanitary behaviour."

Ty had no response. How could he defend himself? How could he when he knew, right now, that he smelled somewhat like an untended pig pen. He had let his usually shaven pubic hair grow in, and the hairs down below had begun to turn a yellowish brown as the sweat and filth that accumulated there tainted them.

His place was in a state of disarray that he had never imagined a place that housed him could ever be in. But he just couldn't bring himself to get up and clean, or do much of anything. He could barely get himself to be as upset as he should have been about what was coming out of the French-Canadian's mouth. What he knew was just another in a long line of rejections. Shunnings.

"Listen, Tybalt... I know of your work situation. And of your... therapy. I do not want you to think of this as au revoir, but it has been decided that it would be best if you remain away from us until you return back on your feet, yes? We can discuss membership then, oui? How does this sound?"

The questions were rhetorical. Tybalt didn't have the words with which to answer them even if they hadn't been. By the time he gathered himself enough to speak, he realized there was no longer anyone on the other end of the line to hear him.

And, just like that, he was out. Really and truly on the outside.

NEVERMORE

i.

He was outside. On the ground. It was raining. Twilight. He was laying on his back beneath a gray and cloudy sky, the last light leaving it. His view of that sky was partially obscured.

Blocked by a bird.

A death-black raven. It was perched on his chest, pecking out his tongue.

Tybalt found that he couldn't move, all he could do was scream for this to stop. But each time he screamed the raven consumed the sound, eating the exclamation, swallowing it and growing larger as a result.

He screamed, it grew, and the pecking only became worse, chunk after chunk of his tongue ripped from his mouth like worms from the ground. The bird slurped and suckled at the sorrowed sounds of Tybalt Ward.

After the bird had grown to the size of a small dog, Ty wised up and bit his tongue, or would have had he still had one. He forced himself to become as still and silent as he could be. Even as the bird rummaged in his mouth, now at the stump of his tongue. Tearing. Rending.

From this angle, Ty could see one of the bird's oversized black eyes. He looked into a black orb that was like a Wizard's Glass.

Inside of that black eye of a black orb of Wizard's Glass, Tybalt saw Tyrone.

Tyrone, the boy Tybalt had once been, was inside of that onyx oculus. Banging on the eyeball from the inside, his hands were mangled bloody twists and bends with shards of bone poking through skin. He was trying to call out to Tybalt, but

Tybalt couldn't hear what the young him, the old him, was saying. He couldn't make a sound to ask Tyrone to repeat himself because the bird would eat that sound and grow and grow and swallow him whole.

Tybalt watched as Tyrone shouted. He saw the young man's wrist snap against the eyeball, but still he pounded on. And even though Tybalt couldn't hear Tyrone, he knew what the young man was saying. Just one variation or another of the word 'help!'.

Tybalt lay there, helpless and unable to help. Not knowing what to do, unable to do anything.

Then came the hands.

Dozens of them, reaching out of the darkness, snatching at every free part of Tyrone, gripping and digging in. Hell's Hands all over the young man just barely graduated from being a boy. Red hands with fingernails that were really blackened fangs. They bit into Tyrone hungrily, pulling him back and away from the glass eye window which allowed him to look out at a view of his future self.

All at once Tybalt could hear the old him, the young him. He could hear the boy inside of his head. A foreign but familiar voice. It said,

"You could have done more once. You could have done better before you moved into your master's house."

The hands, they pulled at him, they tore at him. From him they removed portions.

Tyrone let them. The Hell Hands had not only captured him, they had defeated him. Subdued him. Tyrone stood there with more of his insides being exposed each second, his mangled hands hanging limply by his sides. He only looked at Tybalt and mouthed the words that Tybalt could hear as a swelling in his head.

"Look what has become of us."

A black fanged hand flew to Tyrone's face, fish-hooking him at the mouth, yanking back until the young man's cheek was pulpy rubble.

Still, Tyrone continued to mouth words to Tybalt through his shredded face. Words that Tybalt heard inside his mind.

"Look what has become of us."

Another hand removed the young man's mandible. Plucking it like a drumstick from a chicken leg. Gore fell like rain out of a downspout from what remained of Tyrone's lower face. His bloody tongue swirled and wiggled curiously, unfamiliar with such exposure. Still, he continued to lick at the air, sending words to Tybalt through time and space and life and death.

"Look what has become of us."

One of those hands reached into Tyrone's mouth, which was really no longer a mouth but now a permanently open entry leading to much softer things. The hand began to claw through the roof of what had once been his mouth, reaching for the gray matter beyond that roof. To scramble it. But, before those teeth for nails could enter into Tyrone's brain, he said a final thing, an ending statement to himself. Through words distorted and warped by pain and hurt and torture, he said,

"Look here. Now. See what you have turned me to."

The hands took him, and all that was left was the obsidian black eye that was suddenly a mirror into Tybalt. The bird had stopped pecking. It rose up and looked at Tybalt with eyes as black as Hellfire's scorch.

The rain pounded down on its feathers. As he stared into its black eyes, the Raven reflected back onto Tybalt, allowing him to see into himself. What he was. What he had somehow become along the way.

The Raven waited. Waited for Tybalt to recognize the thing he was inside.

Tybalt did eventually recognize what he was being shown. Within those abysmal black eyes he saw himself and wished he hadn't. Because the sight made it so he could not help but to scream. And scream, he did.

His screams swelled the bird to the size of the world.

His own shouting woke him. Ty opened his eyes to the darkness of his bedroom and, for a horrible moment, thought he was trapped inside of the black eye of a giant bird. He scrambled for the lamp on his nightstand. When he couldn't immediately find it, his idea of being trapped in a large glass eye strengthened. He began to shriek as he waited for black fanged hands to tear him to pieces.

Eventually, he found the lamp. Then there was light. And with it came a slight reduction of his panic.

He saw his surroundings and felt at once relieved and repulsed. He was in his room, but his surroundings weren't really his. What his life had turned into wasn't really him. He looked around at the clothes scattered everywhere. Tissue everywhere. There were bottles of urine, and container after container after container of partially emptied yogurt beside his bed.

He had at first put the yogurt cups into a bag and sealed them tight lest they attract the flies, but the gnats would show up in his bedroom a few at a time no matter what he did. He had used bug spray. Bug bombs. Nothing worked. He saw them, even then, crawling on the lightbulb, attracted to the sudden light. He had begun to take them as a sign. He wouldn't be able to sort out his life until he dealt with them, and everything else that was bugging him at the moment.

Ty couldn't remember the last time his sheets had been changed. He saw that they were discolored from his frequent night sweats, this night's included. He observed the crumpled pieces of tissue paper all over the place, the shoes not on their rack, the disarray that was so opposite to him that it hurt his heart to see it. *What have I turned into?* The question burned in his mind, feeling more like a memory than a thought, but he couldn't recall ever having asked himself that question before today. He had always been proud of the man he had become. Always believed he was destined for greatness. Now he was seriously questioning who he truly was. And where he truly belonged.

The gnats, he told himself. *Get rid of the gnats and you'll get back to you. Clean up and start over. Get back to you.* He would do just that, he told himself. Tomorrow. A fresh, new Monday.

This was a month after that last conversation with Raynaud Bedard.

For the last month he had been in his room, his mobile device his main connection to the world. He checked it only when he absolutely had to. When it was some piece of correspondence that would save his job and his status and his role as a potential permanent member of The Fold.

He had only left his home to buy yogurt and see Dr. Sundra Lucroy twice a week. A few days earlier, he'd had his final appointment. She had done depravities to him. And he had done things that he hadn't thought he would have been capable of doing with a woman that looked like her. That felt like her. Worst of all, that smelled like her.

He hadn't been able to, originally, but she fixed that with her prescription pad. She had written so many prescriptions for Ty – for his Depression, his Agoraphobia, his Anxiety, his Narcissistic Personality Disorder, all of the many diagnoses that had been uncovered in the time he had been her patient. But the prescription most crucial to both of them was for the little blue pills that she insisted he only take on the days of their meetings. Pills that made him able. Made him able to perform. Made him able to separate himself from his penis during those times. And that was bliss, that separation.

The chemicals made him hard. Made it so he didn't have to work so hard at getting and remaining that way. He was able to think of anything he wanted, avoiding the fact that he was now some living sex doll to this woman. This quack who was so in violation of her position over him. This extension of Mr. Johjima's cock.

He had done what he'd had to do. And as he'd done it, he had reminded himself of one of his most important mantras. Number 8:

Do the things that need to be done when you need to do them.

Mantra 8 wasn't just about avoiding procrastination. It was about doing the things that needed to be done even when you didn't want to do them at all. There were so many things Dr. Sundra Lucroy had made him do that he hadn't wanted to do at all. But he had sucked it up and had reminded himself of another mantra of his. Number 6:

Do not allow the things which you cannot control to take control of you.

Yes, he had lost his control, had less control than he'd had since his name had been Tyrone, but he knew that, if he waited it out, he would get that control back. And he would get Dr. Lucroy back as well. Vengeance. He would pay her back for the depravities. And it would all start tomorrow.

Tomorrow was his scheduled meeting with Mr. Johjima. To speak of his progress and potential reinstatement.

He would shower. *Really* shower and not just let the water fall over him as he usually did when he had to meet with Dr. Lucroy. He would wear his best suit, and he would be there early. He would strut, he would preen for the first time in what now felt like years. He would remind them all of who he was.

This Monday would be Tybalt Ward's redemption.

He was a Helping Hand man. A man worthy of The Fold. And tomorrow he would prove that. He would go and get his job back. He would set things right, he told himself.

And after that, he would buy a lot more bug spray.

ii.

"The report says that your heart wasn't in the sessions, Tybalt. It was as though you were always distracted and never focused. This made Doctor Lucroy wonder about your effort level. Even now I can tell that you have not been able to take care of yourself. The arrangement was for you to get therapy and get back on your feet. What have you accomplished since we last spoke here?"

"I... I went to the sessions... I'm clean. I'm here." Ty didn't like the whiny quality of his voice, but he couldn't help it.

This was not how it was supposed to go.

He sat in the main conference room of the Helping Hand office. In front of Mr. Johjima.

Unlike the first time he had sat directly across from the man in power, this table was brimming full of people, none of whom were there to support Ty. These were all people under the payroll of Johjima and Helping Hand. The room was filled with associates and lawyers and other official looking types who did nothing to make Ty feel comfortable. And worst of all, *she* was at the meeting. Ty hadn't been expecting that.

He had washed thoroughly. Had gotten himself ready. He had made it through all the swarms, and he was here. He was here to get his job, not for more questions.

This was not how it was supposed to go.

He had done so many things. So many unspeakable things with that flabby, smelly woman and all of the parts of her she had wanted him to touch with his tongue. He had tried so hard not to retch each time because he knew that it would look bad on his report.

And this was not how it was supposed to go.

He was a Helping Hand man. They were supposed to bring him into The Fold. It wasn't going the way it was supposed to, but there was still time. Time to shine... Time to preen? Ty struggled to remember what it used to feel like to want to be in this position, to want to have the spotlight on him. He was so far removed from that man that the idea of trying to become him once again made Ty want to bolt. But he wouldn't. He hadn't come so far – done so many things – to turn away or be turned away.

He thought about the last question that had been asked of him, pondered what he had done or accomplished during his time away. He could think of nothing. He hadn't even finished reading his hero, Doctor M.R. Johnson's motivational book. How was it possible that he could have been so much of a useless lump for so long?

He tried to think of an acceptable response, anything. Sweat ran down his face like liquid tendrils of a monster come to pull him away. Remove him from all he had ever known, never to return again. He felt it all slipping away as the sweat ran down his cheeks, down his back, pooled in his shoes. Everything he had worked for, he felt it all turning into the same nothing he had accomplished during his time off.

"I went to the sessions..." Ty repeated feebly. Mr. Johjima sighed, folded his hands together and sat up straighter in his chair. He had the air of a judge about to deliver the verdict of a case that he believed to have been a waste of the court's time to begin with.

"Mr. Ward, you smell like a campground." A couple of the others in the room stifled laughter, stealing glances at each other as if gleeful that Mr. Johjima had said what they had all been thinking.

"I've been using a lot of bug spray recently." He didn't want to say more. He saw them casting strange looks, could already imagine what thoughts were behind those expressions.

He had been spraying his apartment with all sorts of bug poison since they had first showed up at his place. *Them.*

Today he had decided to wear the spray like a cologne while away from his home.

"Ah, yes. You called our man about your bug situation. He said it was one of the more unusual inspections he has had to make."

Ty's face grew hot. He had been foolish to call one of their connections. That meant more access to him. More information about the way he had recently been living that he did not want them to have. But they did, and now they were judging, and the verdict would not be good. He was about to be sentenced to exile, and this was *not* how it was supposed to go.

"Doctor Lucroy..." Mr. Johjima motioned to the woman sitting by his side. She was wearing her favorite red blazer with the shoulder pads. A blue shirt beneath it. Her hair was something awful piled on top of her head, and her teeth looked more crooked than usual. Tybalt could barely look at her. He wondered if she had added Therapy-related Post Traumatic Stress Disorder to the list of his diagnoses. Mr. Johjima continued, "...believes that your progress has stagnated. You have not made the necessary improvements in the requisite time allotted to you."

"I went to the sessions! I did everything that was asked of me." Ty was disconsolate. Didn't know what to say or do, yet he continued to babble hoping some of the right words would shoot out of him in the correct order. But nothing was right, Ty felt truly lost. Felt that he didn't know who he was or if he would ever be who he once had been again. Ty heard his voice breaking down. He felt his mouth trembling in a way that reminded him of when he'd been a boy who had just been told his father had died in the war. Tybalt's mouth continued to tremble just as it had back then, and, to his unending horror, he realized that he had begun to cry.

He barked out sounds that were meant to be words but sounded like some sickness to his ears.

The sickness of the weak. It had finally gotten him. A contagion he had long believed he'd grown immune to. Dr. Lucroy spoke, ignoring his tears and whatever mindless noise was yipping and growling out of his mouth. In her obnoxious Scandinavian accent, she said,

"But you were never quite there, Mr. Ward. You were never quite focused in the way that is necessary for a full recovery. Even now I feel like you are not truly with us..."

He only heard roughly half of what she said. He was distracted by something squirming at the corner of her lips.

A gnat crawled out of her mouth even as she spoke.

That was Ty's main issue with Dr. Lucroy. She was full of those things, and they smelled so bad. He had ignored the other bugs he had seen on her during their sessions because he had wanted to be polite, but they were about to fire him and the time for niceties was over.

If he couldn't get his job back, he would at least get that fucking gnat.

Ty leapt across the table and swatted at the bug which had just emerged from Dr. Lucroy's mouth. The result was a resounding **slap!** as his palm connected with her face.

The entire room fell silent.

He looked at her face, looked at his palm.

No bug. No bug. No gnat.

But it's here somewhere. He was sprawled on his stomach on the table, barely registering that Dr. Lucroy now had her palm to her face, the pain setting in once the shock had dispersed. Others had begun to move as well. Some away from Ty and the table, some towards it.

Ty only had eyes for the gnat.

He saw it now, on Mr. Johjima's face. It must have hopped there when he had tried to get it off of Dr. Lucroy.

He knew his hand would be too slow if he tried to swat it again, so he reached into his pocket and pulled out a can of bug spray. He carried one in every pocket on the rare occasions that he left his house these days. He wasn't going to go unprepared again.

Ty saw the gnat leap off of Mr. Johjima's face, but not before he had already depressed the trigger of the insecticide and blasted Mr. Johjima directly in the eyes.

Somewhere in the background, sounding like it was far off in the distance, miles away, Ty thought he might have heard a scream that sounded vaguely like Mr. Johjima, but he couldn't be bothered with that.

He spotted the gnat flying, avoiding the toxic cloud, heading toward the door.

Ty jumped off the table and ran in pursuit.

Two of Mr. Johjima's guards moved in front of the exit to stop him. They had raced to cut him off, standing between Ty and the doorway, him and his enemy.

At that moment, in his mind, came a thought that he believed to be completely logical,

They're trying to protect that gnat. They're trying to stop me from killing it!

Ty didn't calculate this time, didn't wait to relax before he acted. Diminished or not, his body was a weapon. He simply launched it.

There was a flying knee. A Superman punch. A spinning backfist. A roundhouse kick that was punctuated by a sound like an axe catching the trunk of a tree squarely.

Two bodies hit the floor.

Ty would never remember any of this. Not the specifics. In his mind there had been a gnat he had to kill, and a few larger things had needed swatting before he could get to it.

He jumped over the two prone bodies before running out of the room after the gnat. He didn't notice Mr. Johjima fall to the ground clutching his eyes. Didn't hear the old man calling out in Japanese for help. Ty just kept on spraying after the gnat as he ran down the hallways, down the stairs and out of the building into the open air.

He gasped. Panted. He had been catching the blowback of the fumes throughout the entire chase, and the fresh air was a relief he hadn't even known he'd needed. He looked around but couldn't see the little fly. Couldn't see any of them. But that didn't matter, he knew where it would be. He knew where all of them would be. And once he got rid of them everything would be fine. Everything would go back to being okay.

He went in the direction of his home, moving at a pace that was more than a walk but less than a run. He was eager to get there, but he had to make a final stop first.

GNATS

ii.

Tybalt was nearly in a panic as he stood outside of the door to his own condominium unit. He had an infestation, and no one was taking it seriously. No one was taking anything going on in his life seriously.

Tybalt, on this day, less than an hour after chasing one of the pests out of the Helping Hand office, had decided to take matters into his own hands. He had bags in those hands, six of them. Inside three of those bags were bug related purchases, dozens of cans of bug spray, fly strips, bug zappers, fly swatters, citronella candles, things of the like. In the other three bags in his right hand was plant life. Venus Fly Traps. He hoped he had arranged them in such a way that they hadn't been killed on his trot home from the garden center where he had acquired them. The cashier had looked at him sideways when he'd asked her to place the plants in the bags, but she had done it nonetheless. And he had purchased an amount that would ensure he'd have enough survivors regardless of the casualties. If there were casualties, they would be the first in this war. This war between Ty and the gnats. A war that Ty had been afraid of until today, until he realized that nothing had been right since that first tiny fly had shown up on his pillow.

It was like it had crawled inside his head and... he didn't want to think about it.

Do not allow the things which you cannot control to take control of you.

Which Mantra was that again? Ty didn't remember. Didn't care.

He had let them burden him for too long, those pesky flies. Trapping him in his room. Showing up everywhere.

Ruining everything he'd had going with Sakura. Even interfering in his last chance to get his job back. He had seen them everywhere, yes, but this was where they lived. And this was where they would die. Ty was sure of that.

He stopped in his frantic state for only a moment. Just long enough to figure out how to open the door without dropping the bags and stalling his momentum. He expected them to be on him the second he walked in, and he didn't want to wait around thinking about it, losing his confidence.

They usually left him alone as they buzzed around and crawled on the walls, reminding him that this place was theirs, no longer his. He would typically tip toe around, not wanting to disturb the thick patches of them all over his walls. But Ty had a feeling that if he opened the door at this moment, on this day, they would attack. They would somehow *know* he was ready to annihilate them, really and truly this time.

He opened the door with his foot, not kicking it in, but using his foot to manipulate the lever-like door handle that led to an apartment he never bothered to lock anymore. Oddly enough, he had started to think of the gnats as his security force. Anyone who entered his apartment unwanted would walk out once they saw the horror it had become.

There would be no walking out for Ty, however. Not until his task was completed, he told himself.

His goal was win or lose on this day, and he did not plan on losing. Not again. Not on the day he had actually allowed himself to cry.

The memories of his rise and fall kept bludgeoning him.

He would take back this apartment. He would wrestle back the last thing that he could still think of as his. He hoped this would be the first step toward rising again.

With the door slightly ajar, he shouldered it far enough open to squeeze in, then he closed the door behind him and prepared himself to be swallowed by the swarm.

iii.

The only thing Ty was swarmed by was surprise. His apartment was empty, seemingly bug-less. No flies. No gnats. No black patches of moving life crawling on his walls. No winged insects fluttering to and fro in their daily routine. The place was his. Or so it seemed.

He had fallen for this before, when the last inspector had refused to fumigate the place. His condo unit had seemed essentially clear while the exterminator had been there, but moments after he left, the things had crawled and hopped and flown back out. They were a bit more hostile towards Ty on that day, buzzing around his head, several of them following him into his bedroom. It was their way of hinting he shouldn't try something like that again. Their way of expressing annoyance at having to hide.

He had cowered from them that time. But not today. Not now. Not when everything was on the line.

They're smart, a voice in his head reminded him. *They're smart enough to wait for you to make a mistake. Be careful. Be careful.*

Ty decided to play their game. He had expected to come in, guns blazing. Winner take all. But he would play the slow game. The strategy. A chess match.

He dropped the bags in his left hand by the shoe rack before tending kindly to the array of Venus Fly Traps in the other bags. Of the twenty-four he had purchased, six of them were now the compost of the future. He took the remaining eighteen and began to strategically set them up all over his condo.

Four Fly Traps were placed in the kitchen and dining room, that's where the gnats seemed to gather most. Three in the living room. Two in the foyer. Two in the bathroom. Three on the balcony. Four in his bedroom, one of which was right by his door.

The Venus sentry.

He hadn't spotted a single insect as he secured the premises, but Ty would not be fooled. He was still on high alert.

He felt rejuvenated as he grabbed the other set of bags he had left by the front door, spreading their contents all over the apartment as well. He was a man with a renewed sense of purpose. Returned to him was some of his old fight. His spunk. His gumption. That energy stayed with him as he turned his entire condo into an anti-bug battle ground.

And when the battle lines were drawn, as though sensing that the time for war was upon them all, Ty heard a low droning sound coming from his kitchen.

He was in the living room, thankful that he had lit and placed citronella candles at the entryway between the kitchen and where he stood. He thought to himself that if they made it past the Venus Fly Traps, they would be toast at this entry point. And if they made it past this point, he would ward them off with the sprays, and shoo them toward the fly paper he had strung up all over his apartment like birthday party ribbon. And if the Fly Traps and candles and spray and fly paper all failed? Well, he had a pair of fly swatters and a ton of endurance.

The sound of them was like a battle horn. The droning, almost somnolent buzzing of so many tiny flies grew louder as they made their way into his vision. Some of the freshly restored energy and optimism drained out of Ty as he saw them all. Never had he seen so many at once.

He stared in awe at their numbers while his mind was stuck on the question of, *Where could they all have possibly been hiding?*

He removed his blazer and took a few paces further back into his living room. The Venus Fly Traps obviously hadn't worked, and Ty watched with diminishing hope to see if the fumes from the candles would slow them, or if they would be stalled by the fly paper everywhere.

The swarm barrelled past everything he had set up to deter them from entering.

And now Ty stood with them across from him and nothing in between. Waiting. In his dress clothes, his shirt untucked and not all buttons buttoned, sweat stains under his arms, down the center of his back, at his sternum.

Waiting.

Heart racing, chest tight, legs trembling, arms flexed in anticipation. Waiting.

Waiting.

It took minutes for the last of them to come around the corner from the kitchen, the tail of this massive living buzzing collection of a creature. A beast of a swarm. Everything he had seen until this exact moment, he understood to have been a tease. A glimpse of their true strength. They were mobilized now, and they had a collective aim. Him. Their number, if counted, would have led one to madness before allowing one to reach any sort of reliable sum. Millions, he estimated. An army that his Venus sentries were consumed by. An army that blew by the fumes of his citronella candles unphased.

They came at him like a cloud of drifting black filth. Then, yards from him, the slow-moving swarm stilled, and simply hovered. The swarm droned in a way that made sound itself a living creature, one which proceeded to slide into Ty's ears and nibble away at the soft bits inside.

He stood his ground, an aerosol can of insect poison in each hand. He had twenty more on the couch behind him. He was ready to reload and reload and reload once the first two were emptied of their fumes.

Reload and reload until his flooring was black with their felled bodies.

Time seemed to slow down as he drew, using both cans at once, remembering every Western he had ever seen or read or heard about.

These were his six shooters. This was his high noon.

The black mass hovered in front of him, several feet away. This time it was doing the waiting. Though not for long.

Ty sprayed.

Both cans were pointed straight ahead of him as he let out a double burst of toxic anti-insect fumes. When these were empty, he turned to his couch, grabbed two more and sprayed again. The swarm that had been a clump in the middle of his living space had dispersed. They flew everywhere around him. He noted grimly that they all seemed to avoid the fly paper ribbon that decorated his ceiling for this poison party. Still, he was heartened by their reaction to his six shooters. He enjoyed watching their formation break down.

Tybalt laughed and sprayed as he heard what he thought was a collective scream from the swarm of insects. The droning sound had grown high pitched and pained. He laughed some more until he noticed a section of the insects break away entirely and regroup to form a smaller swarm of their own. This new swarm flew to the single light that was on in the apartment. Ty had turned off everything else other than the light in the living room in order to attract the flies. To bring them to him. He saw them covering that light now, and knew this was not a matter of attraction.

This was them wanting to leave him in the dark.

He dropped the two canisters in his hands and went for two more. He still had the light from the sun coming in through the blinds on the windows and door that led to the balcony.

He turned and sprayed with two full cans. The bugs were moving in the air in thick patches. In a way that was almost tactical.

By the time Ty went for two more cans, he noticed the light had dimmed considerably. Not just the light covered by gnats inside his living room, but the late-morning light that had been shining into his home. He thought, at first, that it was maybe about to rain, that the sky might have become overcast. But when he looked out of his windows and his sliding door, he saw that it wasn't cloud cover slowly taking away his light, but more gnats.

More flies, from the outside, pummelling his windows like sheets of driving rain, pressing and milling and crawling all over the glass surfaces, overtaking them. Turning them from transparent to opaque. Threatening to leave Ty in utter darkness.

His distraction by the gnats blocking out the sunlight allowed for the insects inside of Ty's home to gather back together, to re-establish their swarm. All except for the gnats who had dedicated themselves to removing the only light he had. The bugs outside continued to storm the glass, approaching in such numbers and with such force that Ty felt the windows shake. They hit the window panes like torrential rainfall, if rain was made of flying, swarming insects. Insects with intent.

He wanted to breathe deeply but held his breath instead.

Do not allow the things which you cannot control to take control of you.

Ty went back to the couch. Pocketed as many spray cans as he possibly could. Took a full canister of spray in each hand and prepared to fight them off in the total dark. But, before the last light left, Ty saw what the swarm inside of his living room was becoming.

They had collected together in a peculiar way. A particular way.

In the fading light it seemed to him that the swarm had taken a very specific shape.

The shape of a woman.

Then there was no light.

Tybalt closed his eyes, held his breath, and sprayed and sprayed and sprayed.

Post-Mortem

APPLAUSE

We look four months into the future. We've travelled there. Four months after Tybalt Ward decided to wage all out war against the gnats that had so infuriated his life. Tybalt hasn't come along for the ride, but Mr. Henry Johjima has.

We find him in front of a studio audience. He is sitting in front of an array of cameras, which means that at some point he will also be sitting in front of a good portion of the world.

He is on a panel with five women. Five television personalities and him. All of them seated at a table that is part of the set of the daytime television talk show, *Let's Chat*. And what they are chatting about are the events which took place in and around the Daphnis, Washington branch of Helping Hand Home and Auto Insurance several months past.

They are chatting about death of a specific sort.

"You sound very forgiving of Tybalt Ward, Mr. Johjima. Even though this is all widely purported as being his fault. I mean, he rode his employees into the ground, sometimes literally." one of the women on the panel said. Some audience members laughed nervously at this. "He nearly killed two of your security guards – broke the jaw of one of them – and slapped his therapist in the face, who is a woman *By. The. Way.*" Admonishing mumbles, severe whispers, a few jeers. She fed off of the energy of the audience and brought her point home. "He even blinded you in one eye before his death. Yet you sit here and speak on his behalf the same way you speak about young..." she quickly glanced at her cue cards "...Reese Mitchell and Bethany Helmsley."

This was the host, Fredericka Garrett. Mr. Johjima looked at her dark brown skin and short, blonde hair and wondered if she had filled some ethnic studio quota, or if she had slept her way there. Maybe both.

He paused before answering her. His hand instinctively went to the eye patch that had become part of his everyday attire. He went without it when he was not in public, but he was well aware that the cloudy, rheumy muck that was now his right eyeball could be less than appealing to most.

He had been on this media tour since being released from the hospital. It had been months of dealing with social and standard media, speaking about Mental Health Awareness and the importance of being a supportive employer to his employees.

He had hoped to teach Tybalt Ward a lesson in humility. A lesson in discretion. He had wanted to show the young man who was boss, and how to be boss. He hadn't expected him to lose his mind so completely. Mr. Johjima had been disappointed more than anything else when he had heard about Tybalt's death.

He had received a call from the head concierge of Ty's condo, a man connected to The Fold. Mr. Johjima had known of the Sales Manager's end before Ty's own next of kin. The word 'suicide' had been whispered in Mr. Johjima's ear before the coroner had made it official. The first thing he had asked of the concierge was whether or not there was a suicide note. If there had been, and if it spoke of the treatment that he had insisted that Ty undergo at the hands and feet and other parts of Dr. Sundra Lucroy, then Mr. Johjima, Dr. Lucroy, Helping Hand, The Fold, all of it would be at risk. But Ty hadn't left a suicide note, and Mr. Johjima was greatly relieved by that.

Even without the note, suicide wasn't a difficult conclusion to jump to based on the last several months of Tybalt's life. The suicides of two of his subordinates, his recent mental decay (corroborated by Dr. Lucroy's notes), the state of his usually pristine condo unit, and the nature of his death made it safe to assume that the man had taken his own life.

Residents near his unit had complained of a man screaming with maniacal laughter and of a noxious smell. Some immediately near the unit had fallen ill. A family had called Poison Control when two of their young children became stricken with bouts of nausea and vomiting. Poison Control vacated Tybalt's floor and quickly found the source of the noxious gas.

It was bug spray, leaking out of the unit owned by Tybalt Ward.

Inside, they had found Ty. His corpse. It had fallen to the floor of his living room. Nearly two dozen empty cans of bug spray were all around the body. The apartment had been flooded so vigorously with insecticide that the entire place was filled with it. The coroner would later remark that it was amazing the man had lived long enough to empty that many cans while he breathed in their toxins at such close range.

Chemical suicide was the official statement beneath 'Cause of Death' on Tybalt's Death Certificate. What had cemented this determination was the fact that there had been no evidence of insects inside of the man's apartment.

This, to Mr. Johjima, was the most surprising part of all of the events which had unfolded. The fact that Tybalt Ward, of all people, had taken his own life. Mr. Johjima had thought the two had shared the same values on the subject. He had thought Tybalt was made of stronger stuff. Despite the man's skin color, Mr. Johjima had believed that Tybalt could have risen up and done great things, just as Johjima himself, once an ostracized foreigner in this land, had done. Alas, that had proven incorrect. All of the promise of Tybalt Ward had officially been wasted when he was announced as the third suicide within the same branch of Mr. Johjima's company in only a few months. This meant damage control had become necessary once again.

Mr. Johjima was here now, controlling damage, making the best of three bad situations. He was on this talk show to promote mental well-being. He was there to talk about the benefits of therapy, and reaching out to loved ones for help, and calling all sorts of suicide prevention hotlines, the numbers of which had been drilled into his memory by his Public Relations team. They had wanted it to seem as if his advocacy, his encouragement of seeking out help, was second nature to him and not just some knee-jerk reaction. He played the part of innocent advocate well.

Meanwhile, when he used the word Depression, what he actually thought was:

These are just people who are lazy, and not bold enough to make fate their own.

When he used the word Anxiety, what he thought was:

These are just cowards who have found a way to diagnose common fear and lack of bravery.

When he used the word Suicide, what he thought was:

Good riddance.

The mantra of *Survival of the fittest* had been one that Tybalt had espoused and publicly lived by. Mr. Johjima had encouraged the no-nonsense, callous attitude Tybalt had brought to the sales floor. To his life. He hadn't expected Tybalt's method of management to backfire in such grand fashion. He certainly hadn't expected the usually strong and steadfast man to quit, and to stop attempting to survive once he had done so.

Suicide. Mr. Henry Johjima scoffed internally.

He had never expected that Tybalt of all people would succumb to this spreading weakness. To this need to die rather than fight and live.

Weaklings, all of them, is what he thought. But what he said was,

"It is so, so important that we look for the signs of mental health decay. It could be something as simple as a change in someone's appearance. Someone who shaved all the time suddenly looking disheveled and homely. It is important to ask, 'How are you?' in such a way that you truly mean it. And it is okay to not accept 'okay' or 'good' as an answer. Ask follow-up questions. Much of this can be resolved if people understand that they are not alone. It is important for us to believe that others truly care.

"To address your statement, Mrs. Garrett, this is not the time to blame and accuse. That would be pointless now. There is still much healing to be done in the Daphnis community, which is not dissimilar to many communities around our country, and the world. I cannot hold a grudge against Tybalt Ward. I only wish I could have found a way to help him. Now I can only do my best to help others not wind up the way he did."

He held for applause. Received the applause he had held for. Henry Johjima was a veteran of many media scrums and press conferences.

"Due to my strong belief in Mental Health Awareness, I am pleased to announce that we will be opening several Safe Spaces across the country for those who are struggling with their battle against mental illness. These will be places where people can stop by and access on-the-spot therapy. Where they can benefit from activities and engagement designed to de-stress and help them handle crisis situations. We plan to open our first Safe Spaces – each of which we will refer to as a 'Helping Hand House' – next year in Seattle, Washington; Daphnis, Washington; and Tacoma, Washington. Each will be named in the memories of Reese Mitchell, Bethany Helmsley and Tybalt Ward, respectively. We hope to be across the continent within the next decade."

More applause.

It was important for Mr. Johjima to make the audience, both in the studio and all across North America, especially where his company wrote insurance risks, believe that he cared. He had donated several million dollars to Mental Health related causes since these tragedies began. Every mental illness you could name, he had donated a sum to some organization that was interested in ridding the world of it. He knew it was wasted funds; he also knew it was a tax write-off. What was most important of the things he knew was that these donations and TV appearances, the opening of the Helping Hand Houses, and this shovelling out of so much horseshit, were all integral to not only getting his company to bounce back from all of the bad press coverage that Tybalt had brought him, but also to get his company to heights it had never reached before. They would truly be a Helping Hand in the community. And his philanthropy would become incredibly profitable in the long run, his lawyers and accountants had guaranteed. Philanthropy is the newest form of marketing, they had assured him.

The audience responded to his words with great approval, cheering and smiling and clapping and even standing while they did all of this. Mr. Johjima sat there, basking in it all. He would eventually make millions from these Snowflakes. He would turn their sympathy and empathy to profit. To money and assets. Eventually, he would get his eye replaced (he had one of Tybalt's eyes on hold. Waiting). Keeping himself this way was just another piece of strategy from his PR team. Being half-blind had a way of drumming up more public sympathy. Sympathy which would eventually lead to increased wealth for him. For The Fold.

Mr. Johjima did his best not to smile too broadly. It was all going perfectly.

The only thing ruining this perfect moment for him was the small flying insect that was floating there in front of him, a nuisance. He slapped at it, catching it between his palms and taking satisfaction that he had killed the annoying thing.

But when he opened his palms to look at his kill, he saw nothing. He glanced up in time to see the host sparing him a peculiar glance. He continued to slap his hands together, pretending that he had been clapping to begin with, joining in with the audience, hoping no one else had seen his odd movement.

While they all clapped to Helping Hand and its accomplishments, Mr. Johjima discreetly searched the area around him, looking for the gnat he was so certain he had killed.

33 Mantras for Mindfulness and Mastery

Based on the Writings of Doctor M.R. Johnson

1. Rock bottom is just another place to bounce back from.
2. Survival of the fittest.
3. Calculate. Analyze what has happened; formulate what happens next.
4. Recalculate. Check your work. Being correct in the present only helps with being correct in the future.
5. Before you act, inhale and exhale until you're relaxed.
6. Do not allow the things which you cannot control to take control of you.
7. Early is on time, on time is late, and late is unacceptable.
8. Do the things that need to be done when you need to do them.
9. The word 'can't' is overrated.
10. Talk only after listening.
11. Make them feel heard.
12. Focus on the breathing.
13. Say the things you want to do, then do the things you've said.

14. Don't put off until tomorrow what can be done today.
15. Overprepare so you are always prepared.
16. Never apologize unless not apologizing costs you something.
17. Failure isn't truly failure if you've learned from the experience.
18. Hurt is part of the human experience. How one handles that hurt is what defines them.
19. Maintain your composure and posture, always.
20. No matter what situation you are in, make it advantageous.
21. The word risk is the word risk for a reason. Don't beat yourself up for being bold.
22. Without roots there can be no growth.
23. There's always a catch. Don't be caught off-guard by it.
24. Give away nothing.
25. Give away nothing. Literally. Know your worth.
26. Never settle for less than what you deserve.
27. Unnecessary conflict is counterproductive.
28. Exercise your mind as you would exercise your body.
29. KISS – Keep It Simple, Stupid.
30. Separate business from pleasure. Another's pleasure is not your business.
31. Don't let your pride lead to punishment.
32. The most convincing lies usually stem from honest places.
33. Always be on your guard.

Thanks for Reading!

Things haven't exactly gone according to plan in 2020. There was a pandemic, then George Floyd, a black man, was lynched by a police officer, and suddenly there was a bit more pressure placed on everyone with any sort of a platform to speak about things that matter.

I wrote Bug Spray in 2019 when I hoped 2020 would be a year for boundless positive change and optimism, and while that hasn't exactly been the case, it also sort of has been. I am glad to see that many of the topics that I attempted to indirectly broach in this book are now more often being spoken of out loud, and amongst a far more diverse group of listeners. This, to me, is heartening. And as a black author, it gives me hope that me and people who happen to look like me will have a legitimate chance to share our stories and perspective. And that's pretty cool.

But what do a bunch of ghostly gnats have to do with anything? Well, we all have our gnats. *Them*. And sometimes they threaten to swarm. If you are struggling with mental health issues, please reach out to a professional, search for a crisis hotline in your area. Talk to someone. You are not alone, and it doesn't have to be a showdown.

I'd love to hear your thoughts, questions and/or concerns about what you've just read. Please review and rate Bug Spray on Amazon, Goodreads, Instagram, Facebook, YouTube and/or wherever else the humans view the things you post. I can't express enough how important this is to us fledgling authors.

Thank you in advance.

– DIMARO

Acknowledgements

It was easier to write this section of the book the last time around. Since then, I have received more support and encouragement than I had expected, and it has made the process of releasing "Bug Spray" something I have enjoyed, rather than the anxiety fueled panic that was mainly my life leading up to the release of "How To Make A Monster".

So, to everyone who showed up at my first book signing to hang around so that I wouldn't have to sit there sweating and contemplating every life choice I've ever made, I say thank you.

To everyone who took the time to read Bug Spray when it was in its rougher stages and helped me to create the book that you've just finished reading, I say thank you.

And to everyone who has purchased my work, has sent me a message complimenting my stories, has shared anything of mine, or has taken the time to leave a review, I say thank you.
I truly appreciate everything you all have done for me so far.

An additional thanks to Alessandra Sztrimbely, for her editing as well as her perspective.

To Ryan Livingstone, one of my oldest friends and a lifelong source of encouragement. Thank you. And five more minutes for…

Also, as always,

For Fred.
Forever.

Raveena and The Black Man In The White Trench Coat also appear in ...

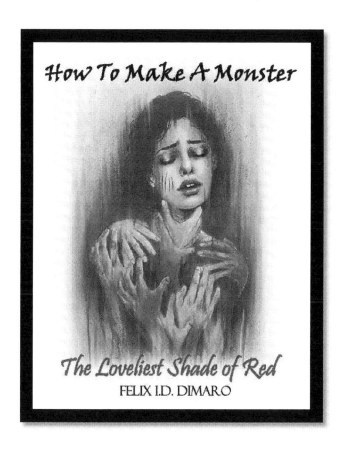

You can find this Anthology of Nightmares on Amazon.

Manufactured by Amazon.ca
Bolton, ON